Time to go.

So why wasn't Cassie moving? Why was she standing there, in front of Joshua, still looking up at that face that was striking even in the dimness of the night?

And why was he still standing there, too? Looking down at her with eyes that seemed to be memorizing her every feature?

It occurred to Cassie that even though they might not have made it to her doorstep, this was exactly what she'd pictured happening if they had. A good-night kiss felt like the next step. But that couldn't happen. She was doing her job. And he wasn't interested in her as anything more than a tour guide and to help maintain the role he was playing.

Yet there they were, still standing there, eyes on each other, and if he leaned only a tiny bit closer....

CELEBRITY
BACHELOR

VICTORIA PADE

SPECIAL EDITION

Published by Silhouette Books

America's Publisher of Contemporary Romance

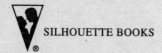 SILHOUETTE BOOKS

ISBN 0-373-24760-5

CELEBRITY BACHELOR

Books by Victoria Pade

Silhouette Special Edition

VICTORIA PADE

is a native of Colorado, where she continues to live and work. Her passion—besides writing—is chocolate, which she indulges in frequently and in every form. She loves romance novels and romantic movies—the more lighthearted, the better—but she likes a good, juicy mystery now and then, too.

Chapter One

"Cassie, I need to enlist you for special services."

Cassie Walker had been called at home and asked to come immediately into the office of the dean of Northbridge College. It was eight o'clock on a Sunday evening and there had been urgency in the summons, two things that had aroused her curiosity.

"Okay," she said tentatively, sitting somewhat stiffly in one of the two visitors' chairs in front of the dean's desk.

"I want you to know that I'm speaking on behalf of myself and Mayor McCullum, because this is a matter of interest to him and all of Northbridge."

"Ah," Cassie said, wondering what the dean could be possibly getting at.

"Are you familiar with Alyssa Johansen?" he asked then.

Northbridge College was a private school in the small Montana town of the same name. The total enrollment was a mere 237 students. Cassie had been an academic adviser and the coordinator of residential advisers for the dormitories since her graduation from the college with a master's degree four years earlier. She wasn't friendly with each and every student, but small colleges were like small towns—she was familiar with most of the names and faces.

"Alyssa Johansen," she repeated. "She's a freshman. Not from Northbridge." Which was why the eighteen-year-old stuck out in Cassie's mind. The school didn't get many out-of-state students. "I've spoken to her a couple of times since the semester started. But I wouldn't say I actually know her yet. It's only been three weeks, though I know she hasn't been in any trouble at her dorm."

Cassie couldn't imagine what about the pretty, vivacious, black-haired girl required the dean—on his own behalf and that of the mayor—to call her in on a Sunday evening.

"Alyssa Johansen isn't really Alyssa Johansen," Dean Reynolds revealed as if it were a state secret.

"Who is she?" Cassie asked.

"She's Alyssa *Cantrell*."

"Alyssa Cantrell," Cassie parroted. "As in Joshua Cantrell?"

That wouldn't have been her first guess had it not been for the dean's emphasis on the name.

"Yes," the dean confirmed.

No one who picked up a magazine or a newspaper or stood at a grocery store checkout where tabloids regularly splashed pictures and headlines could have avoided knowing who Joshua Cantrell was. He was the Donald Trump of tennis shoes: the Tennis Shoe Tycoon, as he was referred to.

"Alyssa is here as Alyssa Johansen to keep her identity secret so she can have some privacy and a normal college experience," the dean explained. "There are only a handful of us who know who she really is. She's Joshua Cantrell's younger sister. His *much* younger sister. He raised her. And the press hound them mercilessly."

The dean paused a moment for effect, then said, "There have been distractions arranged to keep reporters and photographers from realizing where Alyssa actually is—it's very important to her and to her brother that her real identity and her presence here be kept strictly confidential. But, as you know, Parents' Week begins tomorrow. Many out-of-town family members are actually arriving today or tonight."

"Right," Cassie said, fully aware of that fact.

"We had planned for Kirk Samson to do what I'm about to ask of you. After all, he's head of fund-raising. But Kirk was cutting a branch off a tree in his yard late this afternoon when the ladder he was on tipped over. He fell to the ground and hurt his back. He had to be taken to the emergency room and be X-rayed, and his wife called us only an hour ago to say that he's on pain medication and muscle relaxants and will be laid up at least the whole week."

"I'm sorry to hear that," Cassie said.

"So we need you to fill in in a hurry," the dean announced.

"To fill in on what? I don't know anything about fund-raising," she pointed out.

"As I said, it's important for Alyssa to have as normal a college experience as possible," Dean Reynolds said without addressing Cassie's question or comment. "Having her guardian—in lieu of her parents—attend Parents' Week is part of that. Plus, her brother plays an active role in her life and wants to be here with her and for her. He's taken steps to keep the press from following him for the time being, but I need you to show him around. To be his private escort."

The request sounded slightly seedy to Cassie and the dean must have realized it after the fact because he amended it. "What we need is for you to be the school's delegate. We can't have anyone high-profile do it—like the chair of the board of regents or the president or the chancellor or even me. It might cast Cantrell into the spotlight and negate whatever it is he's doing to throw people off his trail. But we want someone with him as much as possible to be his private guide to the school and the town. To make him feel welcome. At home. Comfortable. To make him feel like one of the Northbridge family."

"You know I just closed on my house," Cassie reminded. "My things are all in boxes. I need to buy furniture. To get settled in. I was planning on using every minute I could spare to do that."

"I know you're busy," Dean Reynolds allowed. "But

whether your boxes get unpacked this week or next won't really make much difference, will it? It's important that Cantrell get the personal touch so he feels favorably toward the school and the town."

"I don't know," Cassie hedged, not thrilled at all with what was being asked of her. For more reasons than simply because she had boxes to unpack.

"We need you," the Dean insisted. "You're folksy. A homegrown daisy. No flash. No flutter. One of us, through and through—exactly who should represent us."

Cassie didn't know what *flutter* was, but when it came to flash, she knew she didn't have any of that. Oh boy, did she know it! Not having any of it had cost her a lot.

But that plain, folksy, lack of flash that she personified made her feel all the more unqualified to contend with someone like Joshua Cantrell, let alone impress him the way she was afraid the dean was hoping she would.

"I think you should ask someone else," she said then. "I'm reasonably sure I'd disappoint...well, everyone." Just the way she'd disappointed another important person in her life. "I think you *need* someone flashier than I am."

But the dean wasn't budging. "We just want someone nice and knowledgeable. A welcoming type of person."

But it would still mean being in the company of a man who was a celebrity of sorts. A very attractive, wealthy, well-traveled man. Someone Cassie knew she would be uncomfortable and extremely self-conscious around. Someone who would only serve to remind her just how flashless, flutterless and folksy she was...

The dean must have realized that she was leaning

toward standing her ground and refusing because before she could, he said, "Seriously, Cassie, we're in a bind. I'm confident you're the right person for the job. You're the freshman adviser to Joshua Cantrell's sister, so it won't seem odd that you're who we've assigned to him. You're unobtrusive—"

Ah, another quality to add to the list—flashless, flutterless, folksy and unobtrusive. Quite a claim to fame she had going for her…

"—and I'm asking you as a favor to me, please do this," the dean concluded.

The dean had moved heaven and earth to get her grants and scholarships to pay her way through her bachelor's and her master's degrees because he'd known her family's financial position didn't allow for advanced education. So when Dean Reynolds presented what he was asking as a favor to him, she had to grant it. Which he probably knew and had been saving for a last resort.

"I suppose I can show him around," Cassie conceded reluctantly.

"Good enough," the dean said victoriously. "Now, could you get right to it? Joshua Cantrell is with his sister in the faculty lounge and I want to introduce you. I also need you to show him to the old chancellor's cottage. We've had it cleaned and repaired and updated so he can stay there."

"You want me to meet him *this minute?*" Cassie said, the alarm she felt echoing in her voice.

As a rule, she would not have gone out looking the way she did. But she'd only closed on her house on Thursday and she and her family had spent this weekend moving her in. When the dean had called and asked that she come to his office right away, she'd tried to explain that she was hardly presentable. But the dean had said he understood that she'd been moving and that it didn't matter how she looked. So she'd taken him at his word and had come just the way she was. But now she took stock.

Jeans with a rip in the knee. Yellow crew-necked T-shirt tucked into them. Tennis shoes that were not Joshua Cantrell's brand. Her thick, chin-length brown hair pulled straight back into a ponytail. No makeup.

She was definitely not dressed to meet anyone for the first time, let alone a hotshot like Joshua Cantrell.

But it seemed as if she had no choice. Especially when the dean said, "I don't just *want* you to meet him this minute, I *need* you to. Cantrell and his sister are alone in the faculty lounge and I've left them waiting too long already. I have to get to the mayor's house for a dinner he's having with some mucky-muck from Billings."

"Oh…"

As if that barely uttered word were enough, the dean came around the desk and urged Cassie to her feet, sweeping her out of the office. The next thing she knew, she and the dean were headed up the stairs to the second floor where the other administration offices were.

"We just want Cantrell to like it here. To like the college. To like all of us in Northbridge," the dean was saying on the way. "Let the town's charm infect him. That's all the mayor and I are asking."

Cassie managed only a nervous nod as they arrived at the door to the faculty lounge.

She caught sight of herself in the glass upper half of the door and flinched a little.

She'd been hoping Joshua Cantrell might take one look at her and think country girl, but now she was convinced he would think country *bumpkin* instead. And it didn't help boost her confidence any.

Maybe Dean Reynolds sensed her dismay because with one hand on the doorknob he whispered, "Don't worry, you'll be great."

Cassie couldn't even muster a smile at that. She had experience to tell her that she wouldn't be great at all.

But it didn't matter.

Because just then, the dean knocked once and opened the door.

And there was no turning back.

Chapter Two

The first look Cassie got of Joshua Cantrell was from the rear. He and his sister were standing at the window across from the entrance to the faculty lounge when the dean opened the door and ushered Cassie in.

The girl Cassie had known as Alyssa Johansen—and now knew to be Alyssa Cantrell—was pointing something out to her brother. Apparently they hadn't heard the dean's knock or the door opening because they didn't turn around.

But no matter what the view from the window, it couldn't surpass the one Cassie had of Joshua Cantrell's broad shoulders and expansive back encased in a leather jacket, narrowing to jean-clad hips, an admirably taut derriere and long legs.

"Uh, hmm…"

The dean cleared his throat to gain their attention and this time they heard him. Both Alyssa and her brother turned from the window.

It wasn't Alyssa who nabbed Cassie's attention like a train wreck, though.

Not that that initial vision of Joshua Cantrell's front half was anything like a train wreck. Oh, no, there was nothing ugly about it. In fact, it surprised Cassie considerably. In all the photographs she'd seen of the man in the past several months, he'd looked more like a woodsman than a jet-setter—long, shaggy hair, full beard and mustache. So on the walk up the stairs she'd come to think she was about to encounter a woolly mammoth. A woolly mammoth with an entourage, more than likely—that's what she'd thought.

But not only was Joshua Cantrell alone in the faculty lounge with his sister, he was also clean shaven and his black hair was cut close to his head all over, with only the top a fraction of an inch longer to leave some sexy disarray.

"Sorry to interrupt," the dean apologized. "But Joshua Cantrell, I'd like you to meet Cassie Walker."

"I apologize for my appearance," Cassie said at the conclusion of the dean's introduction. "This is certainly not how I'm usually dressed when I'm doing anything in conjunction with the college, but I've just spent this weekend moving into a new house and I was in the middle of emptying boxes when I got the dean's call, and he didn't really let me know what was going on and—"

That's not the first thing to say when you meet someone!

Cassie silently shrieked at herself when the words slipped out. She cut herself off before it got any worse.

There she was, face-to-face with one of the most awesomely attractive men she'd ever seen in her life and to say she felt even more self-conscious about her hair and the way she was dressed was an understatement. Adonis, meet Dishrag….

And Joshua Cantrell *was* an Adonis.

If there was a flaw in his face, Cassie couldn't find it. He had a square jaw and a chin that seemed sculpted to match; his cheekbones were just pronounced enough to give him a rugged edge; he had a full lower lip beneath a thinner upper that curved at the edges as if he couldn't be easily challenged; a nose that was just straight enough to be masculine and perfect at once; and glorious, crystalline silver-gray eyes that actually seemed to gleam like the reflection of winter snow in steel.

Eyes he cast at the dean in response to Cassie's regretful greeting. "You made her leave in the middle of everything to come here on a Sunday night just to meet me?"

"Oh, it's okay," Cassie rushed to say. "I didn't mind. I just didn't have any idea I was coming to meet someone like you…." She was making it worse. "To meet *anyone*," she amended as damage control. "Or to do anything in any kind of school capacity. If I'd known I was going to be coming into contact with a parent— or a guardian—I would have changed."

"You look fine," Alyssa chimed in. "Like one of us."

There was some truth in that, Cassie realized just then. Alyssa was wearing jeans and a T-shirt, and her brother had on a heather-green Henley T beneath his leather jacket.

"You really do look just fine," Cantrell confirmed, glancing at her again and giving a smile that Cassie had no doubt could wilt any woman's will from a hundred paces.

"Well, anyway," she said, wanting to get beyond all of her opening faux pas as quickly as she could, "I'm pleased to meet you, Mr. Cantrell."

"Pleased to meet you, too. But call me Joshua."

"And I'm Cassie," she said, thinking only after the fact—once again—that that probably had been unnecessary and possibly presumptuous.

"Cassie is the freshman adviser," Alyssa supplied then. "She helped get me out of that awful chem class and into biology."

The dean took over from there. "Cassie has also agreed to be your private guide through Parents' Week. She's good at not attracting attention."

"Kind of like your average, run-of-the-mill, ordinary fence post," Cassie said somewhat under her breath, not appreciating that particular accolade on top of unobtrusive, folksy, homegrown daisy, with no flash or flutter.

Cantrell had heard the fence post remark in spite of her soft utterance, but she was grateful that he didn't comment on it. At least not verbally. The drawing together of his dark eyebrows seemed to refute it, but only in a way that somehow made her feel better.

"Keeping a low profile is the name of the game this week," he said then. "If you can pull that off, Alyssa and I will both be eternally grateful."

"Given the fact that your name and picture are

splashed all over almost everything I pick up, I can't promise anything except that I'll give it a try," she said.

"Good enough."

"Now, if you're ready, I'll have Cassie show you to the house we thought was the best place for you to stay this week," the dean said.

"All right," Cantrell agreed.

The dean returned to the door with everyone else following behind, holding it open for them all. Then he joined Cantrell to descend the stairs, telling him how glad he and everyone else at the college and in town were to have a man of his stature there. Alyssa and Cassie walked slightly behind them.

When they were outside the administration building, the dean thanked Cantrell for coming, assured him Cassie would take good care of him, and then said good-night.

"I should go back to the dorm now, too," Alyssa said when the dean had left. "I have a quiz in my literature class tomorrow morning and I still haven't finished reading the book it's on. Do you mind?" she asked her brother.

"Nah, go ahead," Cantrell encouraged. "I've been on the road all day. I'm looking forward to a hot shower before I crash."

Alyssa stood up on tiptoe and pressed a quick kiss to her brother's cheek. "Thanks. Thanks for coming this week, too. And for everything else you did to pull it off."

"Sure," Cantrell said as if whatever he'd done had been no big deal, even though Cassie had the impression that wasn't how Alyssa saw it.

Still, it was obvious that his sister's kiss and gratitude touched him, and it was nice to see that the ultra-cool titan had a soft spot.

Then Alyssa said good-night to Cassie, too, and trailed off in the same direction the dean had gone.

And just like that, Cassie was alone with Joshua Cantrell in the early autumn evening air, beneath the huge, ancient elm trees that stood watch over the campus.

"Dimples. You have dimples."

"What?" Cassie said after the moment it took her to realize Cantrell's attention had shifted from his sister to her.

"You're actually cracking a smile for some reason and you have dimples," he explained.

She hadn't been aware that his reaction to his sister's gratitude had made her smile.

But rather than showing any more of her self-consciousness, this time she pretended the existence of her dimples was news to her. "No kidding? Dimples? Huh. I wonder where they came from?"

Without missing a beat, Cantrell played along, bending over to take a closer look. "Yep, one in each cheek. Not like any fence post I've ever seen."

Cassie grimaced at that and tried not to notice the magnetic energy the man exuded when he came close. Or the fact that she was not immune to it. She decided against responding to the fence post reference. Instead she nodded in the direction they needed to go—opposite from where both the dean and Alyssa had just headed.

"The dean has you in the old chancellor's cottage. It's this way."

She had another surprise in store for her when Cantrell inclined his chiseled chin toward the school's parking lot. "Will my bike be all right there overnight or is there a place for it at this cottage?"

"Bike?" she repeated, wondering why he'd brought a bicycle with him.

"I came by motorcycle. It's there. In the lot."

Oh.

Cassie focused on the parking lot and there it was. A big, black Harley-Davidson motorcycle.

Despite his jeans, T-shirt and leather jacket, Cassie had still assumed he'd come by car. Limousine or town car, maybe, but by car. Not by motorcycle.

And once more she repeated what he'd said out of shock. "Motorcycle? You came all the way here on a motorcycle? Alone?"

"I was going to come by presidential motorcade but it didn't fit with the low-profile thing," he joked.

"It's just that it's a long way from Billings to here on a motorcycle."

"Yes, it is. Which is why I'm looking forward to that shower."

Cassie didn't know what was wrong with her tonight. She was being so dense. And she told herself to stop it. Immediately.

In an attempt to do that, she searched her memory banks for why they'd started talking about his mode of transportation in the first place.

Parking. And the safety of his motorcycle...

"The chancellor's cottage is at the other end of the campus, so you could park it on the street back there if you wanted, but no matter where it is, it won't be bothered. The most recent car theft in Northbridge was ten years ago and that was more a mistake than an actual theft. Ephram McCain was seventy-nine at the time and got confused because his truck was powder blue and so was Skipper Thompson's. Ephram got into Skipper's and drove off in it—"

"Without keys?"

"Most everyone kept their keys in the ignition until this happened. Anyway, Ephram drove home in Skipper's truck and Skipper reported it stolen. But, like I said, it was really just a mistake and there were never any charges pressed or anything. But if you want to move your motorcycle—"

"No, that's okay," Cantrell said with a slight chuckle. "I don't suppose seventy-nine-year-old Ephram is still on the prowl fifteen years later."

"Actually, he's still going pretty strong at ninety-four, but he did give up driving."

Cantrell laughed more openly at that, shook his head and said, "Just lead me to the chancellor's cottage."

Cassie did that, taking a brick-paved path through the still lush, green lawns of the campus.

At a loss for anything else to talk about, she launched into a campus tour.

"That building behind the administration building—the same flat front, redbrick, only bigger? That's where most of the classrooms are," she began without inquiring if this was information he already had or even wanted. "This whole property was owned by the Nicholas family originally. By the time the parents died, the kids had all moved out of Northbridge and were established in other places, so the Nicholases left the property and all the structures on it to the town to build a college that could mainly serve kids out here in the sticks. The Nicholases' main house is what we use as the dormitory—"

"That old stone mansion," Cantrell interjected to let her know he *was* familiar with that. "Boys in the east wing, girls in the west, with the cafeteria, living and recreation rooms common to them both but keeping the sleeping quarters separated."

"I see you read the brochure," Cassie confirmed. Next, she pointed to the burnished brick building they were nearing. "One of the Nicholas daughters was widowed when she was young and left with three small kids. The parents had that built for her and the kids so they could live nearby. Which they did until the daughter remarried and moved away. It's now our library. The Chancellor's cottage was actually a house for the man and wife who were the Nicholases' domestic staff. It was turned into the chancellor's cottage when this became a college. But only one chancellor has ever lived in it. The first one. He was devoted to the school and never married, so even after he retired the college allowed him to stay in the cottage until his death."

"Did he die in the cottage?" Cantrell asked, for some reason sounding as if he were smiling again, although Cassie couldn't bring herself to glance over at him walking beside her.

"No. He actually died sitting on a brick garden wall

in front of one of the older homes around here. Apparently he'd gone for a walk the way he did every day, had gotten tired and stopped to take a rest—"

"And that was all she wrote for him?"

"He had a heart attack sitting there. No one realized it for a couple of hours. Everybody who saw him thought he was snoozing. He sometimes did that, he'd walk, find somewhere to sit and nap in the sunshine for a while, then get up and finish his walk—"

"How old was this one?"

"Ninety-seven."

"People live forever here."

"Not forever, but we do have some who get up in years. Anyway," Cassie concluded as they rounded the section of the grounds where students often sat on the benches to read or talk, "by the time the chancellor died, the cottage was too small for the current chancellor and his family, plus they were already living in their own home, so the cottage was just left vacant. But the dean says it's been fixed up for your visit."

"You're just full of stories, aren't you?"

"I'm sorry. I know, they're dull," she responded out of reflex because it was what Brandon had always said….

"I didn't say *dull*," Cantrell corrected.

But he also didn't say she *wasn't* boring him, Cassie noted, still convinced that she was.

The chancellor's cottage came into view then, behind more trees and a lavish hedge that was trimmed to just below the paned and shuttered windows.

"It really is a cottage," Cantrell marveled as if that hadn't been what he'd expected in spite of the title. "It looks like something out of Grimms' fairy tales. Not that it looks grim…"

She knew what he meant. The cottage was a small Tudor-style house, with a sharply pointed roof over gables and a front door that was arched on top rather than squared off. The door was also larger than it should have been, dwarfing the house to some degree.

"Are cookie-baking elves going to rush out?" Cantrell asked as Cassie took the key from under the welcome mat and used it to open the oversized door.

Of course it would seem comically quaint to someone like him, she thought as she did. He might be the epitome of the all-American success story but he definitely seemed more like James Dean than Jimmy Stewart.

But she only said, "I don't think cookie-baking elves were part of the spruce-up, no."

She stepped aside so he could go in, but he motioned for her to enter first, earning points for manners even if he had just put down her town. Or at least, that was how Cassie viewed it.

She did go in ahead of him, though, wanting nothing so much as to have this over with so she could get home and not see this guy again until she was more presentable.

He followed behind her as she set the key on the small table just inside the door.

"It's all pretty much here, where you can see it," she said then. "One room. Kitchen, bedroom, living room—"

She did a display-model sort of wave to present it to him and gave him a moment to glance around at the few cupboards, sink, miniature refrigerator and two-burner stove that lined the wall to the left of the door; the sofa, armchair, coffee table, single reading lamp and television beyond that and the double bed, nightstand and chest of drawers that made up the bedroom in an alcove toward the rear of the space.

It had all been cleaned and painted, Cassie noted. Plus there were new slipcovers on the furniture and a fresh quilt over the bed she was betting had just-bought linens on it.

"The bathroom is through that door," Cassie added after a moment, aiming an index finger at the walnut panel facing into the bedroom alcove. "There's a claw-footed tub with a shower over the center of it, along with the rest of the requisite accommodations—nothing luxurious but it's all in working order."

She was just about to ask if he had luggage somewhere when she saw two leather suitcases on the bench at the foot of the bed.

"I guess someone already brought your bags," she said unnecessarily.

"I had them sent ahead. Glad to see they got here."

Cassie ventured to the refrigerator then and opened that door to peer inside, discovering what she'd suspected even though no one had filled her in beforehand.

"The fridge is stocked," she informed him, moving to look in the cupboard above the brand-spanking-new coffeemaker. "There's coffee and filters. And breakfast cereal. Fruit in that bowl on the counter. But I don't see any cookies, baked by elves or not."

He chuckled despite the fact that there had been an edge of sarcasm to her voice.

"Too bad. I like cookies."

Cassie glanced at him then, discovering him smiling amiably enough, clearly unaware that he'd ticked her off. Which probably meant she was being overly sensitive when it came to her hometown—another throwback to other days. To a different man. So she consciously discarded her own minor pique and amended her tone.

"Is there anything you need that isn't here?"

He shook his head. "Seems comfortable enough. I have my cell so it doesn't matter that there isn't a telephone. And I can probably get cookies somewhere else."

He could probably snap his fingers and the dean or the mayor would come running with freshly baked ones, Cassie thought. But she didn't say that. Instead she allowed Joshua Cantrell a small smile.

"Great dimples," he observed with a tilt of that handsome head.

"Mmm," Cassie said, beginning to wonder if the guy was working her for some reason. Maybe he was the kind of man who had to win over and try to seduce every woman he came into contact with. Because surely that could be the only explanation if he was actually flirting with her the way it seemed.

"Tomorrow—"she began.

But that was as far as she got. "Alyssa has only one class tomorrow so she and I are going to spend the day together. You're off the hook as potential-donor babysitter in place of what was his name? Curt or Kirby or…Kirk—that's it. The guy I was supposed to hook up with tonight who already let it slip that he's the head of fund-raising."

So he knew.

Cassie didn't deny it. "Kirk Samson. He hurt his back late today and will be out of commission the whole week."

"Which is why there was the Sunday night phone call to you, dragging you away from moving and not warning you that what they want my sister's freshman adviser to do is take over schmoozing the moneybags."

Cassie flinched and made a face.

"It's okay. Comes with the territory. But let's just do it like this—I know up front what the powers that be want of me. You don't need to put in any kind of plugs or pleas or promotions. Let's just shelve that right off the bat, okay?"

"Okay."

"What *I'm* interested in is getting familiar with the school, the town and the people my sister is going to be in close proximity to and relying on for the next four years. So to tell you the truth, since setting eyes on you, I've been thinking that Kirk the Fund-raiser's accident is a stroke of luck for me—"

"I doubt that it was that for him."

"True. But for me it means that now I get the insider's view. Kind of like going into a restaurant through the kitchen instead of being ushered in the front door and taken to the VIP section. I'm also thinking that if people around here meet me as a regular guy who one of their own is showing around, this will all go much more smoothly. There will be less of a chance of anyone realizing who I am or calling some damn tabloid to report it, and that will ultimately give Alyssa the chance of staying off the radar here. And even if someone does track her to Northbridge eventually, it would help if, by then, your little town likes her—and me—enough to circle the wagons to protect her. I think that could all start now, with you."

In other words, the dean and mayor wanted her to win his favors, and he wanted her to make the whole town love him and form an instant loyalty to him and his sister.

Was that all?

Nothing like a little pressure. And with everything she owned still in boxes she should be unloading.

For the second time—only to a different audience— Cassie said, "I can't make any promises about people liking you or circling wagons to protect Alyssa. But I will show you around and introduce you as Joshua Johansen."

But unlike the mayor, Cantrell seemed satisfied with her reply. "Good enough. I just want a low-profile, low-key, no-big-deal week."

"I'll do my best."

"So tomorrow night? The Welcome To Northbridge College thing?"

"Right. It's a meet-and-greet—mainly with administrators and other parents. The teaching staff will be at the reception on Wednesday night, which you will hear about at the Welcome To Northbridge thing when the dean outlines all of the activities and events scheduled for Parents' Week."

"We can hook up for that, then? After my day with Alyssa?" he asked.

"Sure."

"Great. I'll be looking forward to it."

Cassie wasn't sure if that was simply a courtesy

remark or if he was looking forward to the Welcome night or to seeing her again. There were shades of all three in that simple sentence.

But she opted for discounting the possibility that he'd be looking forward to seeing her because she didn't really believe that could be true.

And since that seemed to conclude what was needed of her—for the moment, at any rate—she said, "If there's nothing else you need then, I'll leave you to your shower."

He smiled again at that and there was a hint of sexy amusement playing about the corners of his mouth that she didn't quite understand. It wasn't as if she'd said something suggestive, she thought.

And yet, once they'd said good-night and she'd left him in the chancellor's cottage, the thought of Joshua Cantrell taking a shower did seem to linger in her mind in a way that wasn't altogether innocent.

In fact, it wasn't innocent at all when she began to imagine him sloughing off that leather jacket, that T-shirt, those jeans....

But Cassie chased the images out of her head by reminding herself that this was Joshua Cantrell she'd been on the verge of mentally picturing in his altogether.

Joshua Cantrell who, if Brandon Adams had been a world away from her, was at least *two* worlds away. Or maybe three or four.

But however many worlds away from her and hers he was, it was enough to remember that he, like Brandon, was not a man for her.

Joshua Cantrell was a successful, wealthy, sought-after man who showed up on magazine covers with a different woman every week.

A different beautiful woman every week.

And she was a country bumpkin.

Oil and water.

They didn't mix.

And she wasn't going to forget it.

Not ever again.

Chapter Three

"Umm, cowboys are coming."

It was late Monday afternoon and Joshua was lying on a blanket he and his sister had spread under a tree in order to have a picnic in the shade. A tree that he'd thought was in the middle of nowhere when they'd pulled the motorcycle off the road a few hours earlier.

His eyes were closed, his hands were under his head and he'd been dozing while Alyssa read her biology textbook. But Alyssa's voice snapped him from the brink of sleep and he opened his eyes to find that two men *were* approaching them on horseback. Complete with the boots and hats to prove his sister wasn't exaggerating when she'd identified them as cowboys.

Joshua sat up, blinked to clear his eyes and then stood.

The two horsemen guided their mounts to within a few feet of the blanket and came to a stop.

"Hi," Joshua greeted.

"You know you're on private property?" one of the men asked without answering Joshua's hello.

"No, sorry, I didn't know. It wasn't fenced off or posted. We were just out for the afternoon, having a picnic. We'll get going, if we're trespassing."

"You're trespassing, but so long as you're not squattin' you can stay a while. Just make sure you pick up after yourself."

"Absolutely," Joshua assured them.

Both cowboys were not much older than Alyssa and might not have been as accommodating had she not been there. But Joshua recognized the interest in the glances both men were tossing in her direction.

Apparently Alyssa hadn't missed it, either. Or the fact that the cowboys were handsome cusses, because she set down her book and got to her feet, too.

"Can I pet your horses?" she asked.

Joshua could barely suppress a laugh at the change in her tone. That was definitely not how she talked to him. But now his eighteen-year-old sister was flirting. And it reminded him that she wasn't a little girl anymore.

There was plenty of other evidence to prove that, as well. She was tall and slender, but had developed some cleavage he'd discovered her showing off underneath the tight tank top and overblouse she was wearing today. She'd also had her black hair cut into a style that was very short and edgy, and she was spiking it on top and in back—something much, much different from the long straight hair with bangs that had always made her look sweet and prim.

There was the addition of makeup, too. She wore a dark gray eye shadow, and a coal-black liner and mascara that caused her pale eyes to stand out much, much more. Plus she was wearing lipstick she hadn't been using the last time he'd seen her, a month ago.

The stuffy headmistress at the all-girls boarding school she'd only recently graduated from wouldn't have approved of the changes she'd made to become the college Alyssa. But Joshua reminded himself that he wasn't her former stuffy headmistress. He was her brother. And he couldn't deny that she was all grown-up. Whether he liked it or not.

So instead of interfering with her playing coquette to the cowboys, he sat back on the blanket as Alyssa went to stand between the horses and their riders.

Joshua didn't abdicate all his responsibilities or brotherly protectiveness, though. Rather than lie down or close his eyes again, he stretched his legs out in front of him, propped one ankle on top of the other, and crossed his arms over his chest, lounging against the tree trunk to keep watch on the proceedings.

His sister's back was to him so only a word or two of what she said as she talked to the cowboys was clear to him. They were grinning down at her and answering her questions with as much coy teasing and flirting as Joshua figured his sister was dishing out. But it all seemed innocent enough and maybe because of that, his mind started wandering.

Well, maybe because of that and because the sight of one of the horses served to prompt his brain.

The horse on the right was a reddish-brown color. Almost the identical shade of Cassie Walker's hair.

Russet—that was what the color was. The color of the horse and the color of the freshman adviser's hair.

Cassie Walker had russet-brown hair. Really stunning russet-brown hair.

Hair so soft-looking, so shiny, that he'd kept trying to will the band that held it to break so he could know how long it was. How it looked when it was free. So he could see it fall around her face...

It had been such a kid-like thing to be wishing for. He couldn't believe he was thinking about her again now—he hadn't been able to think about much else since they'd met, and this wasn't something he'd experienced in all of his adult life. Not even with Jennie. It was a useless waste of the thought process. Of brainpower. And yet there they were, as big as life—thoughts of Cassie Walker spinning around in his head, out of control. As out of control as he'd expect from some horny teenager.

Thoughts and images of her hair, her face, her body...

It wasn't even a remarkable body or a strikingly beautiful face or more than pretty hair. It wasn't as if she had the kind of beauty he encountered day in and day out in the form of fashion models and other amazingly beautiful women who were at his disposal or in hot pursuit of him.

But Cassie Walker had something else. Something all her own...

No, she didn't have the exaggerated cheekbones and

sunken cheeks that were the prerequisites of the models he'd met in his travels, but she did have high cheek-bones. It was just that they were more like little red apples. Little red apples that made her look healthy and full of life.

She also didn't have the surgically precise nose or the forehead that would absorb a photographer's light and cast it back just right. But what she did have was a smooth, flawless complexion and a nose that was small and pert and gave her a sort of air of mischief.

What Cassie Walker had was freshness. And what seemed to him like an inner sunshine that came through a face that was so pretty, so sweet, it just made him want to smile every time he thought about it, every time he pictured her in his head. It made him want to smile the way she smiled. With lips that were just curvy enough, just full enough, just luscious enough, without being overly anything.

And those dimples that appeared when she did smile? He was a sucker for those. They definitely put her over the top.

The dimples and her eyes.

She had great eyes. Turquoise, but more green than blue. Only unlike the stone, her eyes weren't an opaque turquoise. They were luminous and glimmering and had a transparent quality to them.

She wasn't statuesque, either. She was actually on the small side—not more than two or three inches over five feet, he thought. Tiny, almost, compared to the women he was used to. But tight and just round enough where it counted.

He'd liked her. That was the bottom line to it all, and he knew it. That was why he hadn't been able to avoid thoughts like those he was having about her at that moment.

And it wasn't only her looks or her body. She had a touch of attitude that had given him a charge, too. Despite the fact that the attitude had come through when she'd alluded to not being thrilled with the gig the dean had obviously thrust upon her at the last minute.

Attitude and spunk. In a package that might not fit into the category of fashion model, but that defined the word adorable for him.

And if that package were gift wrapped? It would have been gift wrapped in gingham.

Gingham that he might like to take some time to slowly, leisurely, tear away…

"Did you hear that, Joshua?"

The sound of his name brought Joshua out of his fantasy and forced him to pay attention to his sister and the two cowboys again.

"No, sorry, I didn't," he answered Alyssa's question, hoping whatever it was he'd been supposed to hear had been said quietly enough to make it possible that it hadn't reached him.

"They said would you make sure when we leave that the motorcycle doesn't tear up the pasture," Alyssa repeated.

"Sure," he agreed. "No problem."

Satisfied, the cowboys said goodbye to them both then and when Alyssa stepped back, they turned the horses and sauntered off the way they'd come.

"Why do I have the feeling there are horseback riding lessons in your future?" Joshua joked as his sister rejoined him on the blanket, glad to have her company to hopefully distract him from all those thoughts of Cassie Walker.

Alyssa's sunny face erupted into a very pleased grin. "Horseback riding lessons," she mused. "That might be a good idea. Now that I'm in Montana. This is the Wild West, after all."

"Pace yourself, Lyssa. Don't forget you're new to this femme fatale stuff."

Alyssa only smiled.

"You *are* new to it, aren't you?" Joshua probed, wondering suddenly if this was just the first he was seeing of something that had been going on for a while.

"Whatever you say," his sister finally responded as if humoring him. "But don't *you* forget that I haven't been locked away in a convent—even if that *was* how you saw boarding school. It was still in the heart of the French Riviera and there was some fraternizing with other, coed schools and the locals in town. You visited only when you could get away and that left me with a lot of time to fill…."

Joshua grimaced as if he were hearing more than he wanted to hear. "Leave me my illusions," he begged.

"If that's what you want."

"It is."

"Okay. Then we should probably be heading back soon so you can change for that meet-and-greet tonight," Alyssa said then.

"Mmm. It's just so nice and peaceful and quiet out here."

"And with fabulous scenery," she said, glancing at the cowboys retreating into the distance.

"Illusions. Remember my illusions," Joshua reminded her.

Alyssa laughed, obviously enjoying the misery she was causing him. But she went back to the safer subject just the same. "You're sure you want to do the meet-and-greet alone tonight?"

"Yeah, to test the waters," Joshua confirmed. "So far you've made it under the radar on your own, but it's tougher for me since I get splashed around the tabloids more. Before too many people connect us, let's make sure there isn't any initial recognition that might blow it for you."

"I haven't even had a single *you-know-who-you-look-like* here."

"Which is great. That's just what we want. Hopefully I'll get by the same way and maybe we'll be home free."

"I hate for you to have to go alone tonight, though," Alyssa said.

"I won't be alone. I'll be with your adviser. She's been assigned to me by the powers that be who want donations. You know how that goes—I'm sure she has orders not to leave my side."

The idea of Cassie Walker's company pleased him more than he wanted it to. More than it should have, given the fact that it would be against her will. Which, admittedly, was a downer. And yet he was still happy to be going into the evening knowing he would get to see her again.

Then, because he couldn't stop himself and this

seemed like a way of doing it without raising undue suspicion, he said, "So, tell me about her."

"Her? Cassie?"

"Yeah."

Alyssa frowned slightly at him. "I can't tell you anything about her because I don't know anything about her. She's been nice. Like I said before, she got me out of that chemistry class I hated when the instructor wouldn't sign my drop form. She talked to him for me and persuaded him to do it after all. But beyond that—"

"Do you at least know if she's married? Or single? Or engaged? Or involved with someone?"

Alyssa reared back slightly and took a closer look at him.

Joshua knew he was no good at fooling her, but he had his fingers crossed that she might not see through him this time.

No such luck.

His sister grinned ear to ear suddenly, made fists of her hands, raised them and did a little upper body dance, making circles with her fists as she sang, "You like her! You like her! You like her!"

Still hoping to put one over on her, he rolled his eyes. "Jeez, you can be obnoxious."

Alyssa's answer was more of the same torso dance to accompany the second chorus of "You like her! You like her! You like her!"

"I just want to know if I'm stepping on anyone's toes by keeping her away from them. Husbands, boyfriends, fiancés tend to get bent out of shape if their women are having to hang out with me for the sake of work. And if that happens, significant others could take a closer look, realize who I am—and who *you* are—and wreck this whole thing."

His sister didn't buy it for a minute. Instead, she did the dance and the song for the third time.

"Okay, that's getting really annoying," Joshua informed her when she was finished.

"It's true, though."

Younger sisters could be such pains in the neck.

"I don't even know her," he insisted.

"You know she's cute."

"She's just okay," Joshua understated, playing it cool when that one word—*cute*—was enough to bring Cassie Walker's image vividly to mind again. And that vivid image made a ripple of something that almost seemed like delight run through him.

"She's nice, too," Alyssa pointed out.

"I'll take your word for it."

Suddenly Alyssa's expression sobered considerably. "But Cassie's kinda like Jennie. Only worse. At least Jennie was…I don't know, not from Northbridge. But Northbridge is like really, really removed from the kind of stuff that happens around you."

"Which is why we chose the school here."

"And the people are all so…you know, regular. Normal—"

"I do know," Joshua said, feeling a twinge of regret that he and his sister even had to have this conversation, that *normal* and *regular* had become novelties to them.

"You wouldn't risk another Jennie mess, would

you?" Alyssa asked as if it worried her that he might be considering it.

But he wasn't. He wasn't considering it at all. Which was why he absolutely would not act on this interest or attraction or whatever it was that Cassie Walker had set off in him.

"No. Of course I wouldn't risk another Jennie mess." Especially not when just the mention of that name was enough to make him feel guilty and angry and hurt and just plain rotten. "I told you when it happened that that was it for me. That I'd never do that to anyone else ever again."

"You swore," Alyssa reminded him, letting him know she was holding him to it.

Joshua understood. The entire ordeal had scarred Alyssa.

"Because I liked Jennie," his sister added. "And I like Cassie even if I don't really know her. I wouldn't want—"

"Relax. It's not going to happen. I just wondered what you knew about her so I could go in armed. Like if there's someone special in her life, I'd encourage her to bring him along, make friends with him."

That was a lie. Well, the excuse he was giving for wanting to know if there was someone special in Cassie Walker's life was a lie. The rest—the determination not to let anything happen with Cassie Walker—was the truth. Joshua was nothing if not determined to make sure of that.

"It'll be okay," he assured his sister.

But Alyssa didn't look convinced.

"It will," he said more forcefully. "Believe me, after Jennie, I know better. I don't want to go through that again and I sure as hell wouldn't let you go through something like that again, either."

Alyssa nodded, but she no longer looked as carefree and confident as she had earlier. Now she looked very, very young to him again.

"Hey," he cajoled. "Have I ever let you down?"

That made her smile, if only slightly. "No," she answered as if the question were ridiculous.

"And I'm not here to start now. So relax."

She seemed to. Although not completely.

"I want you to be happy," she said then. "It isn't that I don't. I want you to be with someone nice—like Cassie. Someone who would like you for you and be good to you. I just don't—"

"I know," Joshua cut her off once more. "And I'll find someone nice and things will work out. But that isn't what this trip or Northbridge are about. They're about you and your going to college without any hassles. That's all I'm paying attention to right now."

Another lie since the image of Cassie Walker popped into his head yet again.

But still, he meant what he said. This trip and Northbridge were about his sister, about his sister's finishing out her education like any other person her age. It wasn't about his hooking up with anyone. Let alone with someone who had too many similarities to the second-to-the-biggest catastrophe that had hit his and Alyssa's lives.

So pretty or not, spunky or not, even dimples or no dimples, Cassie Walker was—and would remain—

nothing but the woman Northbridge College had appointed as his guide through Parents' Week.

But if things were different, he thought as he and his sister finally decided to return to the small town, if things were different, things might be a whole lot different…

Chapter Four

"On behalf of myself as chancellor of Northbridge College and our entire staff, we want to welcome students, family and friends."

It was the opening line of the chancellor's speech to kick off Parents' Week at the meet-and-greet Monday evening. But as Cassie sat on the auditorium stage with the rest of the advisers and administrative personnel, she wasn't paying too much attention. She'd heard the chancellor make the same speech several times, and she had other things on her mind. Like taking a mental inventory to make sure that tonight—unlike the previous night—when she connected with Joshua Cantrell, she looked her best.

She had on her favorite navy blue pantsuit with the

asymmetrical front-button closure on the short, round-necked, collarless jacket, and the matching slacks that she'd been told more than once made her rear end look fabulous. Three-inch heels with peekaboo toes completed the outfit that always made her feel confident. Which was exactly what she wanted.

She'd had her hair trimmed this morning—not too much, just enough to shape it so it fell to an inch below her chin and swept under at the ends in a way that was neat and professional but had a bit of bounce, too. Plus the style was softened by the bangs that swept over her left eyebrow to add some intrigue.

She'd also been careful to apply a neutral-toned eyeshadow to highlight but not overwhelm her eyes, and two layers of mascara that promised to lengthen and curl her lashes.

The blush she'd brushed across her cheekbones made her look as if she'd spent a day at the beach, and a sort of pink, sort of tawny lipstick had finished her up a mere fifteen minutes before the beginning of the meet-and-greet when she'd left home and come across to the campus.

Maybe not model material, Cassie decided, but she knew she looked better than she had Sunday evening. And that made her *feel* better about herself—which was her goal tonight, even though she was sure it was obvious that she was dressed to impress. To impress Joshua Cantrell.

Not for any personal reason, of course, she insisted to herself. She simply wanted to put her best foot forward for the sake of the school and the town.

Because if she was going to be forced to represent

them both with Mr. Megabucks—whether she liked it or not—she was going to do it at the top of her game. It didn't have anything to do with the fact that she'd gone home last night and dug through her boxes until she'd found a magazine she'd recalled packing, searching for pictures of him. When she'd discovered one— of him pre-woolly-mammoth stage at some benefit with a drop-dead gorgeous underwear model on his arm— she'd torn out his half of the photograph and spent much too much time looking at it.

Paying special attention to her hair, makeup and clothes tonight didn't have anything to do with the fact that she'd gone to bed thinking about him being right here in town. A block and a half away in the chancellor's cottage.

It didn't have anything to do with imagining how she was going to spend the coming week squiring him around. Getting to know him. Getting to see if he was everything he was touted to be when it came to charm and charisma and intelligence and sexiness. Getting to *be* the woman on his arm, so to speak…

No, none of that was the cause for making sure she felt good and comfortable and confident about her appearance today.

Where was he, anyway?

She scanned the auditorium, locating Alyssa Cantrell sitting about six rows back. But Alyssa wasn't with her brother. She had a girlfriend and the girlfriend's parents to one side of her, and a male friend and his father to the other.

Had Joshua Cantrell left Northbridge before the week had even begun? Cassie wondered.

He could have. He could have been called away on business. Or someone could have recognized him and he might have decided to leave before the media got wind of his being here. Or he—or someone he knew or was related to—could have become ill.

Or he could have hated Cassie on the spot and fled before he had to spend another minute with her.

Cassie shied from that notion because it was too demoralizing to consider. Besides, they hadn't exchanged more than a few words last night, and the time they *had* spent together hadn't seemed to go *that* badly.

But even if she didn't allow herself to take any kind of blame, the idea that Joshua Cantrell might have left Northbridge made her feel as if she'd been let down.

Had he left town? she kept wondering as she continued to search for a sign of him in the audience while the chancellor gave the school's mission statement and outlined its goals. Had Joshua Cantrell found a mere matter of hours in Northbridge and minutes with her to be too tedious, too pedestrian, too provincial to tolerate?

He wouldn't be the first man….

But just when that letdown feeling was really taking over, Cassie spotted him.

He was sitting in the very last row, in the very last seat to the left of the stage. Alone.

And that one sight of him lifted her dejection and replaced it with relief and something Cassie didn't want to believe was excitement.

He was sitting off, away from everyone, so she had an unobstructed view of him. For the most part, at any rate— because he was seated, his lower half was hidden. But he had one foot on the armrest of the seat in front of him, causing an upraised knee to be within view where it braced his arm propped on top of it. She could also see that, unlike her, he hadn't gone to any lengths to dress up for this evening. The leg that poked into the air was encased in denim and it occurred to her that it was possible he was wearing the same butt-hugging pair of jeans that he'd had on when he'd arrived in town yesterday.

He had changed what he was wearing on top, though. He had on a tan sport coat over a rust-colored shirt with the top collar button casually unfastened.

Cassie also noted that he was still clean shaven and that his black-as-night hair, while in slight disarray on top, was in an artful disarray that she thought he might have put some small effort into.

Basically, he just looked good. Relaxed. Rested. Sure of himself. And the very essence of cool.

Everything she felt less of now that she'd laid eyes on him again.

But she wasn't going to let him do this to her, she lectured herself with what she'd decided through an entire night and day of thinking about him. She wasn't going to be a basket case around him just because he was some kind of great-looking, sexy celebrity. She was going to remember that she was a well-educated, respected person in her own right, and that he was nothing more than a tennis shoe manufacturer, regardless of how successful a tennis shoe manufacturer he might be.

Still, the reminder didn't keep her heart from beating faster when he seemed to meet her eyes from the distance. It didn't keep her from looking away in a hurry. And it didn't keep her from thinking that this was going to be one very difficult week to get through…

The chancellor wrapped up his speech then. The dean took the podium to read from the handout that everyone had been given as they'd entered the auditorium, outlining the week's events. Once he'd finished that, he invited the audience to have cookies and coffee or tea in the auditorium's lobby.

If Cassie had had any thoughts whatsoever about delaying her second encounter with Joshua Cantrell, it was nixed when the dean's return from the podium brought him directly to her.

"Do you see him?" the dean asked in a confidential voice.

Cassie knew exactly who *him* was, and didn't bother playing dumb. "Yes, I see him."

"Don't leave him cooling his heels. He's important to us," the dean told her needlessly.

"I know, I know," Cassie said, standing with everyone else and following her coworkers off the auditorium stage.

A few people were waiting to talk to someone on the stage as they descended, but most of the parents, friends and family were filing out to the lobby. Joshua Cantrell, on the other hand, had left his seat to stand behind it, but didn't seem intent on going anywhere else, not even to be with his sister. And his eyes were honed in on Cassie as she made her way from the stage to the rear of the room.

"Hi," she greeted as she joined him, sounding somewhat reserved to her own ears and regretting it.

Joshua Cantrell responded by giving her the once-over from head to toe and then smiling with only a single side of his mouth. "I see we didn't pull you away from moving today," he said with appreciation in his voice.

"Monday is a workday," she countered, wanting him to believe she dressed like that every day rather than realize that she would ordinarily have done herself up with such meticulous care only for something much bigger than a Parents' Week meet-and-greet. But she regretted that her reaction to what had been a subtle compliment made it seem as if she were reminding him that being with him was only her job.

Which, of course, was the truth. She just didn't want to offend him by almost blatantly saying that if that wasn't the case, she wouldn't have gone within ten miles of him. So she added, "And you know, tonight is the kickoff to Parents' Week, so we want to make a good impression."

"Done!" he decreed, apparently not having taken offense.

Cassie didn't know what to say to that and opted for moving on. She glanced in the direction his sister had been sitting and said, "Alyssa was over there. Were you late getting here and missed connecting before the chancellor's speech started?"

Cantrell shook his head and Cassie tried not to notice how knock-'em-dead terrific his facial features were. "I wanted to get the lay of the land first, see if anyone seems to know who I am, before people start to associate her with me," he said in a voice that was soft enough for Cassie alone to hear.

"And if someone does realize who you are?" Cassie asked equally quietly, recalling one of the thoughts she'd had when she'd wondered if he'd disappeared suddenly.

"I'll take off and hope I get out before too many people have put us together."

"Ah," Cassie said. Then, because he seemed in no hurry to go out to the lobby to mingle, she ventured the question that had been on her mind since the dean had made his comment about there having been distractions arranged to keep reporters and photographers from knowing where Alyssa was. "Is the haircut and shave part of throwing people off track, too?"

As if just a low tone might not be enough if they were going to say more about this, Joshua glanced around to make sure no one was near enough to hear them. No one was. They were in the far rear corner of the auditorium where no one else had even been seated. And the place was quickly emptying anyway.

But only when he was sure they wouldn't be overheard did he answer her question. "It's something I've done in the past—although not to the extent I've done it this time. We've been planning this since last January when we decided Northbridge might be a place where Alyssa could have the chance to be a normal college kid. I let my hair and beard grow—"

"So the mountain man thing I've been seeing in pictures of you was on purpose?"

He smiled with both sides of his mouth this time. "Kind of gross, wasn't it? There were actually rumors that I was turning into Howard Hughes."

Rumors that had apparently amused him.

"Anyway," he went on, "Alyssa put off cutting her hair when she wanted to, too. Then we registered her at a high-security private finishing school in Switzerland and I paid the school to put her name on reports and rosters to confirm that she's secluded there. I also have someone inside who's leaking information about her to make it look good. Then, occasionally—this week for sure—I'll pay a guy who resembles me and grew out *his* hair and beard, to go to the Swiss village near the school. I have a house rented there and we did a whole clandestine arrival the way I would if I were trying to sneak into town. The guy will mostly stay holed up there except to appear in public periodically to go to the school—dodging the photographers and press the whole time to keep them convinced he's me—"

"And in the meantime, while everyone is looking for a guy with long hair and a beard, and his long-haired sister, you shaved and cut your hair, Alyssa cut hers, and you're calling yourselves the Johansens," Cassie finished for him.

His smile became a grin she couldn't help mirroring as she added, "And you're really getting a kick out of it all."

He shrugged a broad shoulder. "You have to make the best of things."

"Even if the best of things is complicated and expensive?"

"Yep. Whatever it takes. If you can't make light of it as much as possible, it gets to you."

That last part had a more serious overtone to it that Cassie didn't understand. But she couldn't very well question him about it, so she glanced around at the now-empty auditorium and said, "Well, shall we go out and test your disguise?"

"Sure. But first, I had a thought last night that might aid the cause, if you're game. A cover story for you and me."

"You and me?"

"Consider it sleight of hand—if we keep people's focus on the two of us, they'll tend to pay less attention to the connection between Alyssa and me. You know, if I can make you look at this hand—" He raised his right hand in the air and wiggled his fingers. "You're missing what's going on with this hand." He used the index finger of his other hand to brush her hair away from her face.

Cassie understood what he was demonstrating, but if he thought for a minute that touching her—even lightly—was going to be the thing she paid the least attention to, he was *so* wrong. Especially when the bare hint of his fingertip against her face set off little sparks in response.

She pretended that wasn't the case, however, and got back to the point of this. "What kind of cover story did you have in mind?"

"I was thinking we could invent something that put the two of us together—like maybe we were college sweethearts."

"I went to college right here. And this is a small town. More than half the people on the street could probably tell you my shoe size. They definitely know about all my former sweethearts."

"Okay. How about if we say we sort of hooked up on your last vacation?"

"Last year in Disneyland?" Cassie said as if that seemed unbelievable.

Joshua grinned at her again. "You went to Disneyland?"

"I'd never been, so, yes, a friend and I went to Disneyland because we wanted to see it," she said with a defiant tilt to her chin.

He laughed. "Okay. We can say we met waiting to get on a ride, got to talking, spent some time together, you told me about the college and since seeing you again came in the bargain, I persuaded my sister to come here for her higher education."

"You don't have any idea what a small town would do with a story like that, do you?"

"Run with it, I'm hoping. And in the process, keep their eyes on us, gossip about me as Joe Regular Guy who just might be the new suitor of One Of Their Own, and leave Alyssa just an inconsequential afterthought. Like I said, sleight of hand."

"Yes, but at my expense. And I have to go on living here. Answering the questions about you and why you didn't stick around and when you'll be back and if we're serious and on and on and on."

"If I apologize in advance, will you do it anyway? For Alyssa's sake? I really want this to work out for her. Something happened a while back that rocked her—that rocked us both, to be honest—and I want her to have whatever sane time I can give her."

Cassie's students and her own family were important

to her. A plea that hit both of those hot buttons in her wasn't one she could turn down.

Still, she was smart enough not to agree blindly. "How, exactly, would this cover story come out?"

His smile this time was softer, grateful. "We don't want anything that seems forced. But, for instance, when you introduce me to someone you know, if the opportunity arises, one of us can work the cover story into the conversation. It will also make it seem more understandable for us to be together as much as I'm sure we will be this week. Plus I might lean over and whisper to you now and then—"

He demonstrated that as he said it, too, and the feel of his warm breath against her skin caused more of those sparks his finger had set off moments before.

"Or I might touch you a little," he continued. "Innocently. Like here…"

He put a hand on her shoulder.

"Or here…"

He moved that hand to her arm.

"Or here…"

It went to the small of her back…

And with each split second of contact Cassie found it more difficult to breathe.

"Nothing big," he finished. "Just enough to make us look friendly, explain why we're together a lot, and let Alyssa be just one of the kids around here."

Air in, air out, Cassie told herself, consciously breathing and hoping he hadn't noticed that she had been affected by the whisper and the mock caresses.

He might have, though, because then he put that

breath-stealing hand in his jean pocket and added, "But if it bothers you, we can stick with the status quo. It's your call."

She didn't want him to know she could be unnerved by anything so small—which was ordinarily not true. She didn't understand why she *had* been unnerved by something so small when it had come from him. So without much delay, she said, "No, it's okay. It's probably a good idea, even," she admitted, keeping her fingers crossed that when his pretend attentions didn't come unexpectedly she would be impervious to them.

"And actually," she continued, "the story might help appease my family, too. We're very close and I wasn't sure how I was going to explain to them why I needed to concentrate on you this week when they know I planned to duck out of as many Parents' Week activities as I could to unpack and set up the house."

"Great!" Joshua said without further ado, making her think he was accustomed to being granted his wishes and whims, no matter what they were. "Then I feel better about going out into the fray."

"So now you *are* ready to test the disguise?" she asked to be certain.

"To test the disguise and the cover story, if we can work it in somewhere," he reminded.

He took a step backward and motioned with one arm for her to take the lead, clearly intending to stay as much in the background as possible right from the get-go.

Even though she had no idea what he'd been referring to when he'd mentioned something rocking both Alyssa and himself, Cassie assumed it had left him serious about blending in. She accepted the role of decoy and left the auditorium with him following close behind.

The lobby was considerably less spacious and with everyone there now, it made for cramped quarters. Still, Alyssa must have been watching for her brother because not long after Cassie and Joshua got there, his sister found them and urged them through the crowd to meet the students and parents she'd been sitting with.

Cassie noted that Joshua was introduced as Joshua Johansen and she watched for signs of recognition in the faces of the other people. But there wasn't a single indication that any of them doubted Joshua was who he'd been presented as.

That proved to be the case through the entire meet-and-greet and Cassie hoped for his and Alyssa's sake that that had set the course for the remainder of the week, as well.

After about an hour and a half people began to drift out, ending the opening of Parents' Week. Alyssa announced that she needed to read three chapters of biology for her next day's class and when Joshua encouraged her to go back to the dorm to do that, she bid her brother good-night.

Which once more left Cassie alone with Joshua Cantrell.

It wasn't quite nine o'clock by then—not late by big city standards but not early by Northbridge standards, either, so Cassie debated whether to simply usher Joshua to the chancellor's cottage or offer to extend the evening.

In the end, she decided to leave it to him.

"Would you like to get back to the cottage or—"

"Or," he said, jumping at the option before she'd actually given him one.

"Okay. Northbridge doesn't have a bustling nightlife but we could take a walking tour of the town." Which was the only thing she could come up with on the spur of the moment. It might also appease the mayor if he accused her of not doing the promotions he wanted. "How would that be?"

"I'd like it," he said. "It seems like a small-town thing to do. Unless I'd be keeping you from someone— I asked Alyssa if she knew if playing diplomatic envoy with me was driving a wedge between you and a husband or a fiancé or a boyfriend, but she didn't know."

He'd asked his sister about her? Cassie thought, mentally stalling on that tidbit. Had he asked only to make sure he wasn't interfering or because he wanted to know if there was a man in her life?

Not that it mattered, Cassie told herself.

And yet it did matter to her a little. Deep down. She couldn't deny it.

Was it really possible that he had tried to find out if she was single? That the illustrious Joshua Cantrell, man of the world, escort of ladies extraordinaire, was even curious about whether or not the playing field was open with Cassie?

Even the possibility—slight though she was sure it was—boosted her ego.

Still, she tried not to pay too much attention to it and said simply, "You're not keeping me from anyone, no."

"I already know I'm keeping you from some*thing*— unpacking—but if I'm not going to have an angry man tracking me down to do me bodily harm, I'll take you up on that walk."

"No, no one will track you down to do bodily harm," she assured. "There's no husband, fiancé or boyfriend."

Joshua Cantrell's handsome face erupted into a wide grin that gave a second boost to her ego, because it looked nothing but pleased to hear that. "Then by all means, give me the grand tour."

"Tour maybe, I don't know how grand it will be," Cassie said, working as they left the building to contain what almost felt like a hint of glee at the lingering notion that this man—of all men—had wondered if she were free.

And had been happy to learn that she was…

Chapter Five

When Cassie and Joshua left the campus, Cassie led them toward the town square that stood between the college to the west and, to the east, the school compound that educated Northbridge's kindergartners to twelfth graders and offered the town's only sports field.

"Wrought-iron pole lamps that look like they came from Victorian England, and a gazebo. Huh," Joshua mused as he glanced around at the town square's lighting and the gazebo at its heart. "Do you have band concerts here in the summertime?"

Was he making fun? She couldn't be sure. She also couldn't keep the defensiveness out of her voice when she answered.

"As a matter of fact, we do. Along with a lot of other

activities year-round. The square is one of my favorite parts of Northbridge. I love the big trees and the gazebo— I think it's beautiful with its redbrick base and the railing and pillars painted white, and that pointy red roof with the cupola. It's all part of what says home to me."

"I wasn't criticizing," he told her, apparently having picked up on her defensiveness. "I think your town square is great. I like it, too. It's quaint."

Cassie wasn't sure if *quaint* really was a good thing to someone like Joshua Cantrell, but she wasn't going to take issue with him.

Instead, as they crossed South Street to the east side of Main, she said, "Quaint. Well, that will describe most of what you're about to see."

Not all of it, however. Part of that first block nearest to the square had a few more boxy, contemporary-looking buildings and storefronts housing the ice cream parlor and Ling's Chinese Palace—the new restaurant. Plus the government building/police station had a more modern feel to it.

But from the northwest corner of that block, where the old four-story, redbrick former mercantile had been turned into the medical facility, all the rest of the way up Main, the buildings *were* pretty quaint, Cassie had to admit.

Quaint in the best sense of the word, though, she thought as she pointed out businesses, shops and stores that occupied the two- and three-storied, primarily brick structures that gave Northbridge an old-fashioned, country-town feel. Quaint in the best sense of the word when it came to the awnings and overhangs and far-reaching eaves that provided shade and character to most of the edifices. Quaint in the best sense when it came to more of those same town square pole lights lining the sidewalks on both sides of the street, each of them circled with flower boxes that were decorated for the season—planted with white and yellow mums now for autumn—lending that homey, small-town feeling.

Cassie and Joshua weren't the only post-meet-and-greet attendees to graduate to the stroll along Main Street. Several other faces from the college's Parents' Week orientation were out and about, too, to mingle with a few Northbridgers.

Smiles and greetings were exchanged along the way but no one seemed to think any more about Joshua's real identity now than they had earlier, and so Cassie and Joshua were able to take their walk without incident.

They did, however, encounter Roy Webber, the local Mr. Fix-it, and one of the town's biggest busybodies, and in introducing Joshua to him, Cassie included the cover story she'd agreed to.

It clearly pleased Joshua, who nudged her with his shoulder once Roy Webber had moved on and said, "Thanks for getting that out there."

"By tomorrow noon, the whole town will have heard it," she informed Joshua. "Roy Webber is a bigger gossip than any woman I've ever met."

"Perfect," Joshua said with satisfaction. "I owe you."

"Yes, you do," Cassie said from atop her high horse as they made a U-turn at the northernmost end of Main.

They'd gone up an incline to reach what was the formal entrance to Northbridge and as they crossed from the gas station to the bus station, Joshua paused halfway between the two to peer down at the view of nearly the entire town from that vantage point.

"This is nice," he mused.

"Quaint," she repeated a bit facetiously.

"I like quaint. I don't know what made you think that was an insult," he insisted.

Cassie knew she could be overly sensitive when it came to things like that. She admitted to herself that she was probably being harder on Joshua than he deserved for something that was a part of her own baggage. So she tried to get out of the course she'd set with some semblance of aplomb.

"Okay, I'm sorry if I misunderstood."

"Apology accepted," he decreed as if something about her amused him.

They finished to cross the street but Joshua continued to look out at the town, this time focusing on Adz, which stood in the center of the block at the base of the hill.

"Did you say that that Adz place belongs to your brother?"

"I did," Cassie confirmed as they went on at a leisurely pace.

"And it's a pub and restaurant?"

"Right." Cassie briefly considered asking Joshua if he wanted to cross back again and go in for a drink, but the idea of introducing him to Ad and having to explain why she was with Joshua in a social situation wasn't something she was eager to do. So she didn't make the suggestion.

If it had occurred to Joshua, he didn't show it. Instead, he seemed more interested in her family. "Do you have just the one brother?" he asked.

Cassie laughed a little. "No. I have four. One who's my twin."

"*Four* brothers?"

"Four."

"Are you the only girl?"

"Most of our dogs have been girls, but other than them and our mom, yes, I was the only girl. Of course, now Ad has gotten married and Ben is about to, so we're getting a few more females into the mix."

"Where are you and your twin in the lineup?"

"Ben is my twin," she said. "We're the youngest."

"And is… What did you say his name was? Ad?"

"Right. Short for Addison."

"Is he the oldest?"

"No, he's the middle child. My brother Reid is the oldest, he's a doctor—"

"Here?"

"Yes, we're all here. Then there's Luke, he's with the police, then Ad, then Ben and me."

"Big family," Joshua marveled.

"Not a small one, that's for sure."

"And you all live and work in Northbridge. You *must* be close."

Obviously he'd been paying attention when she'd made that comment earlier. She liked that. "We are."

"Dad's not in the picture—you mentioned your mom but not your dad."

"Dad died when Ben and I were eight."

"I'm sorry. How did he die?"

"He was a mechanic and he was working under a car when it fell."

They reached the only intersection that had a stoplight and joined several other people waiting at the crosswalk sign. One of the group was a student Cassie knew and they exchanged greetings.

When the light changed and they could all move again, Joshua veered away from the subject of her father's death when Cassie was only a child. "Believe me, I know how bad things are after something like that," he said before leaving it behind. "But otherwise, how was it growing up here?"

Cassie was only too happy not to delve any more deeply into that dark time in her family history, so she gladly answered the question that altered their conversational course. "I never grew up anywhere else so I can't really make a comparison," she said as they continued their walk. "But I liked it. I think we had more freedom than city kids did—or can—because around here, everyone knows everyone and we all watch out for each other. As a kid, the good part was if I fell off my bike six blocks from home, I knew I could get a Band-Aid just about anywhere. Or a drink of water or a cookie, if I smelled baking. The other side of that coin, though, was that I could never get away with anything. If I was into mischief just about anywhere, I almost always got caught and no one hesitated to reprimand me or threaten to tell my mother—which they usually did."

They were both primarily looking straight ahead or at the shops they passed, but Cassie felt Joshua glance at her then.

When she looked over at him in return, she discovered him smiling at her. "Did you get into a lot of mischief?"

"My fair share."

"So you weren't a prim-and-proper-have-tea-parties-with-your-dolls kind of little girl?"

She laughed slightly at that. "I had four brothers," she reminded him, as if that should have been explanation enough. "My dolls usually ended up as casualties of some war reenactment or monster attack, or their heads were shaved bald or beards and mustaches were drawn on their faces in permanent marker. And a tea party? I would have never survived the humiliation of something so sissy. Mostly I heard a lot of *'Jeez, Cassie, don't be such a gi-rl.'*" She mimicked a lower voice for that last part and made Joshua laugh.

"Being a *gi-rl*—" he parroted her "—was a bad thing?"

"Until my brothers grew up enough to actually like them. Then I became the resident expert. The trouble with that was that if, as the resident expert, I made a bad call on a shirt or a cologne or something else their girlfriends or the girls they were in hot pursuit of ended up not liking, they blamed me for ruining their lives. I was also answerable for every girlfriend's bad mood or tantrum or ultimatum or unreasonable demand."

"You were the everywoman."

"Unfortunately. I was also the missing link, so to speak—whenever a girl wasn't particularly interested in one of them, they were sure I could convince her to like them or they tried to force me to make that girl my best friend so I could bring her home with me and they could wow her with their basketball or football prowess or maybe work in a biceps flex that they were sure would melt her on the spot if only she could see it."

Joshua laughed again. "You lived a life under pressure."

"Four brothers," she said simply.

"I would have thought it would be tougher on your own social life to have four brothers. That they would have run off your dates or scared guys into not having anything to do with you."

Cassie used that as an opportunity to look at him again, wishing the sight didn't make something inside her flutter to life each time she did. "Is that what you've done to poor Alyssa?"

He had the good grace to smile sheepishly. "Once or twice. When I've really thought the guy she was interested in was a jerk."

"Even if she didn't think he was a jerk and really liked him?"

"Hey, we're talking about you and your brothers," he said with mock defensiveness.

Since they'd made it back to campus by then, Cassie saved delving into his relationship with his sister for another time and merely said, "Sure, there were a few guys who my brothers got in the way of, but I didn't stand for too much of that without dishing out some of the same medicine."

Joshua leaned close and said, "Don't give Alyssa the tutorial on that."

Then he straightened up again, robbing Cassie of the warm flush she'd gotten from his nearness.

A warm flush that had instantly fogged her brain.

It took her a moment to get her wits about her, but

when she did, she said, "And that brings us back to the school. You've now seen most of what Northbridge has to offer—with the exception of living accommodations."

"And you probably want to be done with work for today and get home," he guessed as they stopped walking within feet of the curb, in the initial shadow of the campus's first tall, imposing elm.

It was surprising how uneager Cassie was to be finished with work for today or to get home when it meant ending this time with him. But she could hardly confess that.

She did, however, hedge slightly. Just so she didn't seem rude, she told herself.

"Unless there's something else you need me to point out or explain or…"

He didn't seize the *or* the way he had earlier, though. Now he let her off the hook.

And disappointed her a little…

"It's okay, you've served your sentence for today. I have some proposals I should read tonight anyway. Just let me walk you to your car and then you can punch out."

He couldn't have been more wrong in his assumptions that she was thinking of this either as some kind of punishment or as work by then, but she wasn't going to tell him that any more than she was going to admit she wasn't anxious for this to end. So instead, she merely addressed his offer to walk her to her car.

"I don't drive to work. I live right there," she added with a nod over her left shoulder.

His eyebrows arched. "Which one?"

"The second house from the corner at the other end of the block."

"Then I'll walk you home tonight," he decreed.

But Cassie had an instant image of what it would be like if he actually did that. Of saying good-night to him at her door. Of how end-of-date-like that would seem—end-of-date-like enough to picture him kissing her…

And it rattled her.

"No, no, that's okay," she said in a hurry. "We can just say good-night here. The dean would have my head if he thought I'd made you go a single extra step on my account."

"I won't tell him if you won't," Joshua promised with a hint of a smile and innuendo in his voice.

"No, but someone else might," she countered. "Small town, remember?"

Joshua merely nodded slowly, accepting her claim but giving no clue as to whether he was buying it.

"Okay," he conceded. "Then we say good-night here."

But still Cassie dragged her feet…

"Tomorrow night is the football game between the college's makeshift team and the locals. Then there will be a big bonfire and marshmallow roast afterward. Were you interested in that or going with Alyssa or…"

Another *or.* And Cassie had more hopes hanging on it than she wanted to.

"Let's go as a threesome," Joshua said without having to give it much thought. "If that's okay with you. If you don't have other plans or would rather not go at all or…"

An *or* of his own. Cassie was glad he wasn't taking her for granted despite the fact that he knew entertaining him was her assignment.

"The three of us going is perfectly fine with me," she jumped in.

"Great. Alyssa's dance class is doing the halftime show, so I don't know how much of the game she'll actually be watching before or after that. And if you're there, she can bounce between me and her friends, and you and I can make the cover story look good."

"Right. The game is at seven-thirty, so shall I meet you two at the stadium?"

"Whatever you say."

"I'll be there a little after seven, then."

"Great."

And that was it. No more to say. No more *or*'s. Time to go.

So why wasn't she moving?

Why was she standing there, in front of him, still looking up at that face that was striking even in the dimness of the night?

And why was he still standing there, too? Looking down at her with eyes that seemed to be memorizing her every feature?

Then it occurred to Cassie that even though they might not have made it to her doorstep, this was exactly what she'd pictured happening if they had. A moment at the end of an evening spent together, an evening she'd enjoyed, an evening he'd seemed to enjoy just as much, when a good-night kiss felt like the next step.

But that couldn't happen, she lectured herself. This wasn't that kind of situation. She was doing her job. And he wasn't interested in her as anything more than a tour guide and a beard to maintain the role he was playing.

Yet there they were, still standing there, eyes on each other, and if he leaned only a tiny bit closer....

But even if he did, she couldn't let it happen, some latent voice of reason warned her. Work. He was work. He was Joshua Cantrell. She was just Cassie Walker, small college adviser, country girl. Country bumpkin...

She drew her shoulders back enough to make her spine ramrod straight, enough to make her appear less receptive than she thought she surely must have seemed.

"If you need anything before tomorrow night—"

"Alyssa and I will probably take another ride outside of town between her classes the way we did today, plus I have some calls that need to be made, so I'm sure I'll be busy. You don't have to worry about that."

"Okay, then. I'll see you...and Alyssa at the stadium tomorrow night around seven."

Joshua nodded his agreement, his gaze remaining on her just as intently as it had been when she'd entertained the idea of him kissing her.

Still, Cassie knew getting away from there, from that moment, from him, was her best bet, so that was what she did. She took two steps backward and said, "Good night."

"Good night."

She wished he would leave, too, but he didn't seem inclined to do that. She gave him a little wave that she worried afterward might have seemed too coy, too flirtatious and not at all businesslike. But once it was out there, there wasn't anything she could do about it, so she merely turned and headed for her house.

Not until she reached her front stoop did she hazard

a glance in that direction again, feeling certain that Joshua would be long gone by then.

He wasn't, though.

He was still standing right where she'd left him. Watching her. Raising one big hand to belatedly answer her wave, letting her know that watching her was exactly what he was doing.

But why *was* he doing it?

Was he simply making sure she got home all right? Because now that she was unlocking her door, now that he'd waved, he did finally turn to leave.

Or was there more to the last few minutes of keeping an eye on her than mere safety's sake?

Probably not, she told herself. It was probably just the making-sure-she-got-home-all-right thing. After all, he wasn't accustomed to small-town life. He probably had no idea that the crime rate in Northbridge was nearly nonexistent.

And yet as Cassie went inside and closed the door behind her, she was aware of a tiny twitter of pleasure rippling through her.

A tiny twitter of pleasure at even the scant possibility that Joshua Cantrell had gone on looking at her until the last possible moment just because he hadn't wanted to stop…

Chapter Six

"Maybe the cover story wasn't such a good idea," Cassie whispered to Joshua after the eighth—Cassie was counting—woman had climbed to the top of the stadium stands to meet her "new friend" at Tuesday night's football game.

"I think we're still okay. People are just curious about who's hanging out with their hometown girl. I haven't seen any signs of anybody putting two and two together to figure out who I am," he whispered back.

The football game was between a makeshift, volunteer team of college boys and the Northbridge Bruisers—the local team of grown men who kept in shape by playing football, basketball and baseball, depending on the season—and usually only against each other.

Even so, the games always brought out a lot of spectators. First of all, in a small town like Northbridge, any form of entertainment was widely supported. Secondly, the men who *didn't* play still liked to watch the games. And thirdly, one of Northbridge's best natural resources was a high percentage of hunky men, so the female population—particularly the single female population—rarely missed a game, either.

But tonight Joshua Cantrell was drawing equally as many looks and veiled glances and outright stares as anyone on the field. Not to mention all the trumped-up excuses people were coming up with to be introduced to him.

Yes, Cassie did think that a portion of the interest in Joshua came from the story she knew had been well circulated today that a man she'd met on her last vacation had encouraged his sister to enroll in Northbridge College so he could see her again. But it concerned her that the more interest the story inspired and the closer the scrutiny, the better the chance that someone might recognize Joshua.

He was right, though, that that hadn't happened yet. So far everyone just seemed to be checking him out.

And there was an abundance *to* check out, Cassie thought as she sat beside him on the bleachers in the cool late September air.

He was dressed casually in jeans and a blue V-neck sweater with a plain white crew-necked T-shirt underneath it, but he still looked great—effortlessly well-put-together. And there was no denying that he was smoking hot—his facial features were perfectly chiseled, he had terrific hair, and with all of it working at once, he definitely stood out even in the midst of some of the best-looking men Northbridge had to offer.

Plus, the longer Cassie was with him and the more she saw him interact with the people who did come up to them, the more she realized that the man was highly approachable, that he was genuinely accessible, that he didn't have any sort of superiority complex. He seemed like just an everyday guy. Which, she supposed, would aid the cause of keeping it secret that he was a business mogul whose every visit to a restaurant or theater or party or charity event made headlines. But still, his ability to seem like an everyday guy surprised her.

It also made it more difficult for her to keep in mind who he actually was and that regardless of how everyday-guyish he might seem now in this setting, at this time when fitting in was exactly what he was aiming for, he still *wasn't* just an everyday guy. And he was about the last guy on Earth who she should ever have been thinking about in terms of kissing last night.

Joshua Cantrell was a tennis shoe magnate, she had to keep reminding herself. That was who he *really* was. He certainly wasn't her plain, ordinary, small-town counterpart, which was the only kind of guy she had any hope at all of having a successful relationship with.

Even thinking about kissing him was just silly. Supremely silly. It was asking—it was begging—for trouble. Trouble she had no intention of courting for a second time in her life.

It was like the Northbridge Bruisers, she decided as she tried to keep her focus on the game. Those guys— four of them her brothers—didn't aspire to anything more than playing against each other or against other neighboring small-town teams, or the occasional group of college kids who banded together for a little friendly competition. The Northbridge Bruisers knew their limitations, they made the best of them, they enjoyed themselves anyway. Maybe they enjoyed themselves more because they *didn't* aspire to be something they weren't.

And that's me, Cassie thought. She needed to know her limitations, to make the best of them, and only then would she—could she—be happy. She needed to acknowledge that she was not an exciting enough person to be someone Joshua Cantrell would end up with.

Even if she *was* wearing her best heather-gray turtleneck sweater and matching slacks instead of the old jeans and sweatshirt that were her usual Bruiser-watching attire.

Besides, what if Joshua Cantrell kissed as smoothly, as confidently, as adeptly, as expertly, as he appeared to do everything else? It might go to her head. It might cloud her thinking. It might make her forget just who she was after all. And she couldn't risk that any more than she could risk that kissing him might be something she liked so much she'd get hooked on it. Because about the time she did get hooked on it, she knew that she'd lose it. Just like before.

Nope, no kissing. No forgetting her place or herself. That was how it had to be.

But if she were guessing? she thought as she caught sight of him out of the corner of her eye.

Her guess would be that he did kiss amazingly….

"There's Alyssa!" Joshua said then, interrupting

Cassie's thoughts as the halftime show began and his sister marched out onto the field with the rest of her dance class to perform.

It wasn't something that would ordinarily have happened, but the object of Parents' Week was to show off as many of the students' accomplishments and activities as possible, and this was one of the ways that had been suggested. So there they were, doing a number that was a cross between a dance routine and a cheer, to the beat of music blaring from several boom boxes positioned to face the wooden bleachers that lined one side of the field.

The group, mainly girls with only a few boys thrown into the mix, did well and when they were finished, everyone in the stands clapped and cheered, and some—Joshua among them—whistled loudly.

It struck Cassie then just how parental a position Joshua took with Alyssa and it made her curious.

She didn't buy tabloid newspapers, so beyond seeing them at the grocery store checkout with Joshua's face on the covers and name in the headlines, she'd never read what was written about him inside. She *had* read an article here and there in other, more reputable magazines and caught tidbits of gossip on TV occasionally. But nowhere in any of that had she ever learned anything about his background. She'd been only vaguely aware that he *had* a sister but she hadn't ever encountered information about any other family members.

Suddenly she recalled the dean saying on Sunday night that Joshua had raised Alyssa, and for some reason that information sunk in only now. Enough to make her wonder suddenly exactly how that had come about, and why.

She was still wondering about it all when the football game ended with a victory for the Northbridge College boys. But Alyssa joined Cassie and Joshua as they walked from the field to a large open space not far away where an enormous bonfire was being lit, so she couldn't ask any questions.

But once the fire was roaring and Cassie and Joshua had settled onto the blanket Cassie had brought for the occasion and Alyssa had gone with her friends to toast marshmallows, Cassie finally found the opportunity.

"It seems like I'm not the only one close to my family," she observed after Alyssa had brought a paper plate full of the charred sugar pillows for them to share and then returned to the fire.

"Alyssa and me?" Joshua said as he popped one of the confections into his mouth, glancing at his sister in the distance as he did.

"For starters," Cassie responded.

"As far as family goes, it starts and ends with the two of us, now," he said.

"Really? There's *just* you and Alyssa?"

"Just the two of us. For the last eleven years. We lost our parents when I was nineteen, Alyssa was seven."

"I'm sorry. So you know firsthand how bad things are after something like that," she added, referring to the comment he'd made in conjunction with her own life long ago.

"I do," he confirmed.

"I hadn't read…or heard…about that," she said then, not wanting him to think she was merely playing dumb.

"It—like almost everything else I haven't gone to extreme measures to keep quiet—has been out there for public consumption."

"You've gone to extreme measures to keep some things quiet?" Cassie asked, surprised.

"Yeah. Once or twice," he said bluntly, raising his eyebrows in a way that made him look instantly weary and frustrated.

But then the look was gone and he turned his head to watch Alyssa and the bonfire, and Cassie had the impression that whatever it was he'd gone to extreme measures to keep quiet wasn't something he was going to talk about with her.

So she returned to what she'd been curious about in the first place. "It sounds like your parents died together."

He nodded but continued to keep his gaze on the fire. "In a plane crash. My dad sold shoes for a living—wholesale to chain stores. He had to travel a lot and my mom stayed at home to raise first me, then Alyssa. Dad was good at what he did, he was the top seller for years and years on end, and was finally rewarded with an all-expense-paid trip to Las Vegas—"

"From?"

"Cleveland—that was where I grew up. Anyway, I was in college—the middle of my second year at UCLA. But I came home for Christmas break, so they scheduled the trip for that week between Christmas and New Year's so I could stay with Alyssa while they had their trip. The trouble was, I made it to Ohio and we had a nice holiday, but my parents never made it to Nevada. They were flying in a company plane, not a commercial jetliner, and they hit bad weather over the mountains of Colorado. It took three days after we were notified that they'd gone down for the rescue party to get to the crash site."

"That must have been a horrible three days. Was there hope that they might have survived?"

"We weren't given any, but—" He shrugged. "Until you hear the words, you can't help but hope."

Cassie could see reflected in his expression just how much hope—desperate hope—he'd had, and just how difficult that time and the loss of his parents had been for him. Difficult in a different way than the loss of her own father when she was about the same age Alyssa had been, because while she'd suffered through losing her father, she'd done it within the cocoon of her brothers and her mother.

"Was there just you and Alyssa alone, waiting through those three days?"

"There were some family friends with us," Joshua said. "And some of the bigwigs from Dad's company. But as far as family, as far as everything *after* those three days and getting through the funeral, we didn't have anyone. All our grandparents were gone. My father had had a brother but he'd been killed in Vietnam, and my mother was an only child. Alyssa and I were it."

"So there you were, barely an adult, with a seven-year-old sister?" Cassie said, feeling a wave of sympathy for the kind of panic that had to have overwhelmed him under those circumstances.

She saw his gaze seek out his sister as a small, sad smile curved the corners of his mouth. "There I was, not an adult at all, with a seven-year-old sister," he amended wryly.

"I knew—from newspapers and magazines and things—that you had a sister, but I didn't know you raised her. Well, except that the dean mentioned it on Sunday night, but there was so much other stuff going on during the conversation I had with him before he brought me up to meet you that there weren't any details or anything," Cassie explained. "But you really *did* raise her?"

Joshua's handsome face turned to Cassie. "I guess you could say that. But a lot of the time it seemed more like we were raising each other. I didn't start out as the most mature nineteen-year-old on the planet."

"You must have been mature enough to step up to the plate when it came to Alyssa."

Joshua let out a humorless chuckle and shook his head. "I wish I could say that—that I stepped up to the plate. But to be honest, it wasn't that heroic. I was a scared kid who wanted to run the other way. And I almost did." He glanced at the blanket for a moment as if it wasn't easy to look her in the eye. "I actually had my bags packed and a plan to sneak out of the house right after the funerals. A neighbor was staying with us—my mother's best friend—and I was just going to leave Alyssa there with her. Go back to the California sunshine, try to forget I had any family at all left, and never be heard from again."

"You and Alyssa weren't close before your parents were killed?"

"Hardly. With twelve years separating us? I was an only child and she was just an unpleasant surprise my parents sprung on me when I was more interested in playing sports and hanging out with my friends. She was their hobby, I had my own—that's the way I saw it. And her."

Cassie had to smile at his candor. "So why *didn't* you leave her behind?"

He'd caught Cassie smiling and once he had, he went on looking at her again, smiling a little himself now. "I started to think about my mother's friend having five kids of her own. Her husband being out of work. I thought, *What if Sheila doesn't keep her? What if Alyssa just ends up in a foster home or something?*"

"You weren't crazy about having a seven-year-old kid sister on your hands, but you didn't like the idea of a foster home, either."

"That's about it. I'd had a friend in middle school who'd been in and out of foster care. The stories he'd told were grim. I know it isn't all bad, that there are some good ones—my friend ended up in a good one finally, but before that happened, he'd been in some rotten situations. Really, I guess I was still kid enough myself to think about how mad my parents would have gotten at me if I'd have let something like that happen to Alyssa, and even though they weren't around to show their disapproval, I just couldn't bring myself to do it."

"So you stayed."

"No, I went back to California. I just took Alyssa with me."

"What did you do, hide her out in your dorm room?" Cassie joked.

"She was fine under the bed while I was in class, I slipped her water and cookies, and after lights-out I'd let her come up for air."

That was too ridiculous for Cassie to believe. "Funny," she said. "What did you really do?"

Joshua smiled, having enjoyed his sarcasm even if he hadn't fooled her. "There was no more school for me. I sold the Cleveland house, but there was a mortgage on it that the sale barely covered. There was some life insurance on my dad, but none on Mom, and Dad's wasn't enough to set up house for Alyssa and me, pay my tuition and keep us going while I finished school. I had to make a living. My dad's company offered me a job in-house—from guilt, I'm sure—so I went to work with them."

"Selling shoes?"

"I couldn't travel the way my dad had had to do. No, they put me in the manufacturing end, which happened to be headquartered in San Diego. As it turned out, that was the good to come out of the bad."

Cassie was still curious about his relationship with his sister. "So you went to work making shoes—what kind?"

"Ladies' high heels, mainly."

"Not what I expected to hear, but anyway, you went to work making ladies' high heels and raised your sister."

"Like I said, we raised each other. For a while at least. She had to tell me when her bedtime was and then—" he laughed at the memory "—then she'd say, 'Is it eight o'clock yet? Because when it's eight o'clock you have to say for me to go to bed or I'm not going to go, even though I can tell what time it is.'"

Cassie laughed, too. "She warned you to be the parent or else."

"Pretty much."

"And if you forgot to tell her to go to bed?" Cassie inquired.

"She stayed up for a while, then gave me hell about how I was supposed to be taking care of her and taking care of her meant telling her when to go to bed because she was just a *child*—she said it like that and used that word—*child,* not *kid, child*—very dramatically."

Cassie laughed again.

"But eventually I resigned myself to being the boss," Joshua said. "I can't say it came easily or that sometimes we didn't resort to fighting like *two* kids, but things evolved and we got through it. And then, yes, we became very close, and after a while it was the two of us against the world."

"He's telling you the how-he-became-my-dad story, isn't he?"

Cassie hadn't seen Alyssa come up from behind her.

"I asked," Cassie said as Alyssa plopped down on the blanket with them.

"Did he tell you how bad he was at it?"

"Hey!" Joshua protested. "You're still alive and well, aren't you? I must have done something right."

"You should have seen him in the tampon aisle the first time—his face turned so red I thought he was going to pass out," Alyssa confided.

Cassie laughed yet again as Joshua rolled his eyes. "Do you *want* me to talk about the jock strap incident?"

Alyssa beat him to the punch by telling Cassie what he was referring to. "I was thirteen and there was no way I was standing there while he picked out one of *those* things."

"So she made a scene and stormed out of the store like a little diva. That was *sooo* much better than my turning red."

"I was *thirteen*," Alyssa repeated emphatically.

Cassie merely sat back and enjoyed the spectacle of their good-natured bickering. It was something that could well have been happening between herself and any one of her brothers over numerous embarrassments they'd inflicted on each other.

But even as she watched the interplay, she thought that it was very impressive that Joshua—as a green nineteen-year-old and for whatever initial reasons— had taken on the support, care and raising of his much younger sister. And even now, when another man might consider his duty served, he was bending over backward to do what was best for her. Plus, he was participating in Parents' Week—something he could well have begged off of as the busy older brother and not her actual parent.

It struck Cassie at that moment that she was glad he *hadn't* begged off. She was glad he'd come. She was glad she'd inherited the job of keeping him company because she was discovering that he was an interesting man.

Alyssa had moved on to a new subject and Cassie was happy to escape thoughts she knew she shouldn't be entertaining. "…he's the guy I told you about and he lives in town so he's having a bunch of us over to his house tonight. You said you needed to make that overseas call so we weren't going to make it a late night anyway—"

"Go!" Joshua ordered before the list of arguments in favor of Alyssa's leaving him to spend time with a boy got any longer.

Alyssa's pretty face erupted with delight. "Thanks. But if you miss me too much, you can go to the convenience store and buy some tampons to think of me," she goaded.

Joshua rolled his eyes again but Cassie noted that he did not turn red or even appear to be embarrassed. "I think I'll pass, thanks."

Alyssa was still pleased with herself as she got up from the blanket. "I'll see you tomorrow, then. Remember that I don't have classes in the morning, so we can have breakfast, but then I have a lab in the afternoon so I won't be able to do the parents' luncheon."

Cassie had forgotten about the parents' luncheon.

"That's okay," Joshua assured his sister. "Maybe Cassie can walk me through that," he added, unknowingly putting Cassie in a bad spot.

But it surprised her to see Alyssa's expression change with the same comment. The younger girl sobered considerably, and frowned as if she would have preferred to hear that her brother would skip the luncheon rather than go with Cassie.

Why? Cassie wondered, taken aback. She'd thought that she and Alyssa got along very well. She liked Alyssa and she'd assumed that Alyssa liked her. Did

Alyssa not want to share her brother? Even in the superficial way that had been arranged for this week?

That seemed like the logical conclusion and yet something about it didn't ring true to Cassie. If Alyssa was possessive of her brother, why wasn't she making sure she took up every moment of his time here? Instead, what was actually happening seemed more normal. It seemed like what would happen between Cassie and one of her own brothers if the situation were the same—they would spend time together but they would also not be upset over separations to pursue other interests, too.

So maybe she just doesn't like me, Cassie thought, unhappy with that possibility.

Alyssa didn't say any more about the next day, though. She merely said good-night to them both and left.

But Cassie was too stunned to keep quiet and before she even knew she was going to say anything, she heard the words come out. "Does Alyssa have a problem with me?"

Joshua didn't pretend to have missed the alteration in his sister's attitude when he'd mentioned seeing Cassie for the luncheon. "Actually, she likes you a lot," he said without missing a beat. "Which is why she'd kind of like to protect you from me."

Surprise number two.

"Because with women other than your sister you're a low-life scum-dog?"

"Ouch!" he said, rearing back as if he'd been hit. "You haven't read enough about me to know the family stuff, but you *have* read the ugly lies and rumors?"

"Only on the front pages," she said, holding her

ground with a smile, because she was beginning to think that a man who behaved the way he did toward his sister would not be a man who treated other women badly. Besides, his treatment of her had been flawless, too, further discrediting his public image as a womanizer.

"Alyssa isn't worried about my being a dog, no," Joshua said then, clearly not having taken offense because he was smiling, too. "She's worried about what comes along with me. Ordinarily. What we're working so hard to avoid here."

"Is it so bad that she thinks I need protecting from it?"

Joshua's smile dimmed. "It can be," he said with an ominous edge to his voice.

But again he avoided getting into what he apparently didn't want to reveal because he glanced at the dwindling bonfire and the crowd beginning to disperse, and he said, "Looks like tonight's festivities are over and I'd better walk you home."

Cassie reminded herself that she was on the job and should be only too willing to have the job end. It just wasn't how she felt. Again tonight.

It was, however, what she conceded to. "It is getting late and I understand you have an overseas call to make," she said, referring to what Alyssa had said moments earlier. "But you don't have to walk me home. We can walk back together and split up the way we did last night."

"Now that I've seen where you live, I think I can manage the whole walk to your door before cutting across campus."

Short of a reason to insist otherwise, Cassie didn't

agree or disagree. She merely gathered the marshmallow debris to take with her when she stood.

But Joshua beat her to her feet and then held out a hand to help her up.

And again she didn't know how to gracefully decline the courtesy he was extending. So, although she was leery of making physical contact with him when she already knew it set off things in her that were difficult to take in stride, she had no choice but to accept his hand.

The big, strong hand that closed around hers with complete confidence and shot ribbons of warm honey straight into her blood stream.

She'd felt sparks and had problems breathing when he'd touched her in the auditorium just before the meet-and-greet the previous evening; she felt warm honey now. It was definitely difficult to take in stride.

"Thanks," she muttered the moment she was standing and could retrieve her hand, willing herself to ignore the fact that something any number of other men had done in her lifetime with absolutely no noteworthy effect on her could actually make her feel weak-kneed and wobbly when it connected her to Joshua Cantrell.

One of the Northbridge College students came by to collect their trash just then and Joshua took it from Cassie's other hand to drop into the black plastic bag. Then he nodded to the blanket still on the ground.

"You get that end and I'll take this one and we'll shake 'er out and fold 'er up."

Cassie had to laugh at his mimicry of some of the twangs the ranchers and farmers around Northbridge sometimes had, and it helped defuse the potency of his touch.

Still, it was a little sexy having him help fold the blanket when they drew close together, face-to-face, to accomplish it. But Cassie guarded against letting that impact her. For the most part.

Then, with Joshua carrying the blanket tucked under one arm, they set off across the town square with everyone else who was heading back to the college.

"I noticed you didn't jump in when I mentioned the luncheon tomorrow," he said along the way.

He was observant, too. The man had many levels.

"I can go if you want to," Cassie hedged. "But I have to warn you that it's cafeteria food."

"And not only don't you want to eat it, I have the feeling you might have other plans."

He was good. He really was.

"Are you clairvoyant?" she asked with a laugh.

He leaned sideways and said, "If I see that in the tabloids, I'll know it came from you because that's one thing no one else has ever accused me of."

"I promise not to tell."

"So, you're just busy tomorrow?" he persisted.

It almost seemed as if he actually cared. But Cassie thought that couldn't possibly be true.

"I was going to sneak away to have lunch at my mother's house," she said. "She's been gone for the last three weeks on a cruise to Alaska. She just got back today and brought some smoked salmon and moose jerky or something that she wants me to try."

"Even moose jerky sounds better than cafeteria food."

"You could come—" Cassie cut off her own words, for the second time tonight speaking before she thought.

Joshua glanced over at her. "Really?"

"Well, I mean, you probably wouldn't want to, and that's okay, but—"

"Why wouldn't I want to?"

"I don't know. It's not like it's going to be some splashy thing, it's just lunch at my mom's."

"I'd like to meet your mom."

This time, it was Cassie who glanced at him. "You would?"

"Sure."

"Oh. Well. Okay. Does that mean you want to go to her house for lunch tomorrow?"

"Will I be intruding?"

Cassie had to laugh at that. "No. My brothers have brought home entire work crews on the spur of the moment. My mom's philosophy is the more, the merrier."

"Think she'll recognize me?"

"I can't promise she won't. She's a sharp lady. But I do know that if she does, she'll never tell anyone."

"How about the brothers? Are any of them going to be there?"

"Mom's fixing lunch—that's the word on the street—so any or all of them could show up, yes. But the same goes for my brothers—if they do recognize you, they'll keep it quiet."

"So can I come?"

They'd arrived at Cassie's doorstep by then and as she unlocked the door, she said, "If you want to. But seriously, it won't be fancy."

"I'm not a fancy guy," Joshua insisted.

"Okay, then," Cassie consented, glancing up at him in the glow of her porch light and discovering that he looked very pleased with himself.

"Can I bring something?" he asked then, obviously enjoying the prospect of the coming lunch.

"To my mom's? She'd be offended. She's always the provider of the food."

"Good, because I don't know what I'd bring anyway."

"Why do I have the impression that this is funny to you?" she asked when he seemed unable to contain a grin any longer.

"I'm just excited to see you in your natural element."

"Is this an expedition into the wild?"

He leaned slightly forward and whispered, "I'm hoping it's my chance to see you not at work."

She couldn't very well tell him that what he'd seen of her so far wasn't really her at work since every time they were together she ended up feeling more as if she were on a date. So she didn't say anything at all.

Then, he straightened up just as she wasn't sure he was going to and said, "What time?"

"Noon. Shall I come by the chancellor's cottage to get you or—"

"I'll have Alyssa show me where your office is and meet you there before that."

"Okay."

"Okay," he echoed.

With that settled, she thought he'd say good-night and leave. Which was good because while they'd been discussing his going with her to lunch tomorrow, she'd avoided what she'd been worried about the previous evening—this scene at her door evolving into something it shouldn't. Even if it was only in her own mind.

But just when she thought she was home free, he did it anyway.

He leaned forward again and kissed her.

Not on the lips, though. On the forehead.

"Boy, you really aren't anything like your reputation." Strike three—her mouth had run away from her again.

Joshua's grin this time was slow and one-sided. "Disappointed?"

"Well…" she said because now that she'd gotten herself into this, she didn't know where else to go with it.

Joshua, however, did.

Just that quick, he took her by the shoulders, pulled her forward and leaned in to kiss her for real. Mouth to mouth. Agile, supple lips to her shocked ones. Just long enough for her brain to stop spinning and realize that she was actually being kissed by Joshua Cantrell after all.

Then it was over. Too soon to be analyzed or judged or even enjoyed. Especially when she was so stunned.

And there he was, grinning again.

"See you tomorrow for lunch," he said before taking his hands away, turning and leaving.

And tonight it was Cassie who stayed standing there, watching him go. But not to see where he went or that he got there safely.

She watched him go because she couldn't take her eyes off him while her lips were still tingling from a kiss that had taken her completely by surprise.

A kiss she wanted to happen all over again so she could know if it had lived up to her greatest expectations.

So she could experience it with a clear head.

And truly know what it was like instead of feeling as if she'd sleepwalked through something that just might have been even better than she'd imagined.

Chapter Seven

"We're here," Cassie announced as she and Joshua went in the front door of her family home at noon the next day.

She'd called ahead to let her mother know she was bringing someone with her, so Lotty Walker had already been warned that her daughter wouldn't be alone.

Lotty didn't come out to greet them, however. She only responded by calling, "Kitchen."

"Back this way," Cassie explained to Joshua as she led him to the rear of the house into the big country kitchen.

Lotty Walker was adjusting the temperature on the oven and so didn't immediately turn toward them. When she did, she stopped short at the sight of Joshua.

"Oh, Cassie, your friend is a man," she exclaimed, her round face paling slightly and her blue eyes widening. "I thought…it didn't occur to me…you just said you were bringing a *friend,* you didn't say a *man* friend…and I made pigs in a blanket."

Pigs in a blanket was whispered in an ominous aside Joshua could obviously hear because he was standing right beside Cassie.

Cassie understood why her mother was upset, but a confused Joshua said, "Pigs in a blanket?"

Cassie opted for explaining what pigs in a blanket were rather than addressing her mother's alarm. "They're small hot dogs wrapped in dough and baked."

"I know what they are," Joshua said. "But why—"

Before he could say more, a panicked Lotty said, "I'll throw them out right now! I figured you were bringing one of your girlfriends or your secretary. I wouldn't have made them if I'd known you were bringing a man. I wouldn't do that to you again!"

"It's okay, Mom," Cassie was quick to assure her mother. "This is Joshua. Joshua, this is my mom, Lotty Walker. Even if he's heard of them, Joshua probably hasn't ever eaten a pig in a blanket, but it's all right that you made them. He's just a *friend.*"

"He must be more than that. Look at you—you're in your good interview suit."

As if the pigs in a blanket issue wasn't bad enough, Cassie internally cringed at the fact that her mother had just let Joshua know she was more dressed up—again— than she would ordinarily have been. That yes, she was wearing the navy blue crepe pants and matching short, form-fitting jacket that managed to be professional-looking and feminine at once. It was the suit she'd pur-

chased especially for her job interview at the college and
had worn only on important occasions since.

"And your shoes," Lotty Walker pointed out, completing Cassie's embarrassment. "Those kill your feet. You
never wear them unless you want to impress someone.
I'm throwing the pigs in a blanket right in the trash."

Cassie caught sight of Joshua from the corner of her
eye. He was smiling as if this all amused him. He was
also wearing jeans and a gray Henley T-shirt that made
him look casual and comfortable and far more at home
than Cassie did in the modest house with her mother in
jeans and a flannel shirt with the tails hanging out.

But he apparently decided to step in just then and al-
leviate some of Cassie's misery, because he finally forced
his way into the conversation by belatedly accepting the
introduction. "I'm happy to meet you, Mrs. Walker—"

"Lotty—everybody just calls me Lotty."

"Lotty. And please don't throw away the pigs in a
blanket. I *have* had them before. My mom made them
once or twice, if I'm remembering right. For hors
d'oeuvres at barbecues. They're good with a little plain
yellow mustard."

Lotty beamed. "Oh, thank goodness you're one of
us," she said, obviously relieved by that revelation.

Cassie could only smile a pained smile, appreciating
that Joshua had smoothed the pigs in a blanket problem
so adeptly. Appreciating, too, that he knew what pigs in
a blanket were and that, if he considered them some sort
of horrible, low-life concoction, he was hiding it well.

The front door opened just then and a deep male
voice said, "I smell pigs in a blanket."

Cassie couldn't contain her mortification any longer. She closed her eyes and shook her head, opening them to a grinning Joshua.

"What can I say?" she confided. "We're a pigs in a blanket kind of family. You aren't going to get pâté for lunch here.

"Good. I hate pâté. Give me a hot dog over that any day."

In this, if not in anything else, Cassie thought, Joshua might be different than Brandon, and for that she was grateful. She just swore not to let the fact that he hadn't made a big deal out of pigs in a blanket go to her head. He *was* still who he was. She was still who she was. And never the twain could meet.

"Hey," her brother Reid greeted them as he arrived in the kitchen.

Cassie introduced Joshua a second time, realizing only when her oldest brother accepted the other man at face value and didn't recognize him as anyone special, that her mother hadn't, either.

"Reid is the doctor in the family," Cassie explained as the two men shook hands.

"How about you?" Reid asked. "What do you do?"

"Import, export," Joshua said smoothly, clearly having decided on that line as part of his cover-up. He went on to say that he imported some raw materials and exported some of the products that were produced from them, and while he didn't list shoes in particular, Cassie had the impression that importing some of what he used in the making of his tennis shoes and exporting the shoes themselves was the basis of this portion of the tale.

Lotty told Joshua to sit at the table then, and put Reid to work pouring iced tea and Cassie to the task of taking food out of the refrigerator.

"I see more than four places here," Cassie observed on her first trip to the table. "Who else is coming?" she asked her mother.

As Lotty stirred potato salad, she said, "Parents' Week has Ad's business booming so he couldn't make it, and Ben is too busy getting ready for his party tonight—" The older woman looked to Joshua as an idea apparently struck her. "Cassie's twin brother, Ben, is about to start a school for troubled teenagers and he's having an open house tonight, if you'd like to come."

"I might take you up on that," Joshua said, surprising Cassie until it occurred to her that he was probably just being polite.

Lotty continued, "Anyway, Ben won't be here for lunch either, but Luke—" She stopped mid-sentence when her second-to-the-oldest son announced his entry into the house much as Cassie and Reid had. "There he is now," Lotty concluded.

Luke, who was a local police officer, strode into the kitchen just as the timer on the stove went off.

Lotty handed Cassie the bowl of potato salad to take to the table while she retrieved the pigs in a blanket from the oven and slid them onto a serving plate.

Cassie again performed the introduction of Joshua before Lotty ordered everyone to sit.

"Pigs in a blanket, potato salad, baked beans, smoked salmon on some cream cheese and crackers, and that's the moose jerky," Lotty said, pointing to everything on the lazy Susan in the center of the large table. "Dig in."

Cassie spotted Luke looking from Joshua to the pigs in a blanket and back again before he said to their mother, "Pigs in a blanket? Really, Mom? You did it again?"

Cassie rolled her eyes, wondering if she was ever going to escape this subject as her mother said, "Joshua's okay with them."

Reid took pity on his younger sister and said, "So, Joshua, not a lot of importing or exporting in Northbridge. What brings you here?"

Without missing a beat, Joshua told the cover story, causing raised eyebrows to be cast in Cassie's direction.

"You didn't tell us you met someone in Disneyland," her mother said.

"There wasn't anything to tell," Cassie claimed. "I didn't know until Joshua e-mailed me a week before the term started that his sister had actually picked Northbridge College."

"Yeah, right," Luke said, voicing what the rest of her family was obviously thinking—that something more was going on between her and Joshua.

But the *more* they seemed to think was happening was along the lines of a secret romance rather than what was actually happening, and because that was what Joshua had been hoping for, Cassie merely left her mother and brothers to their suspicions and spun the lazy Susan until the moose jerky was in front of Reid.

"You first, Reid. You get to be the moose jerky tester."

Reid spun the lazy Susan in Luke's direction. "There you go, Luke, you do the honors."

"And I'll get the pictures," Lotty announced, leaving the table for the counter nearby. "We can pass them while we eat so you can all see them before you have to go back to work."

Looking at vacation snapshots while they ate—that would have caused problems, too....

The thought came on its own into Cassie's head but she pushed it out again just in time to hear her mother say, "Joshua, you wouldn't be interested in seeing me and my friends on a cruise, but I'll bet you wouldn't mind looking at Cassie's scrapbook."

"No, no, no, not the scrapbook!" Cassie protested while both of her brothers laughed.

"Everybody we bring around has to see our scrapbooks," Luke explained.

"Not Joshua," Cassie insisted, wishing she could say he was only part of her job, that this absolutely was not the kind of personal relationship they were all thinking it was, the kind that made the scrapbooks unavoidable.

"Definitely Joshua," Joshua countered with a grin, accepting the bright yellow album that Lotty had already jumped up and taken from the old oak ice chest where she stored the chronicles of all five of her children.

"Pigs in a blanket and the scrapbook," Cassie muttered to herself, thinking that this lunch couldn't have gone worse. For her, at least. Joshua, on the other hand, was dipping the small wieners in cheap yellow mustard and diving into the scrapbook.

It was difficult for Cassie to pay attention to her mother's vacation pictures, eat and keep an eye on what

Joshua was discovering in the scrapbook at the same time. Plus her mother was going back and forth between explaining the vacation photos and joining Luke and Reid in regaling Joshua with anecdotes to accompany the scrapbook pictures and memorabilia. By the time lunch was finished, Cassie felt as if she'd just run some kind of frantic race. But Joshua seemed to be enjoying himself.

"This one looks pretty recent," he said when he finally reached the last of the filled scrapbook pages at about the same time Lotty brought a container of ice cream and a bowl of fruit to the table for dessert.

Cassie leaned to the side just enough to peer at what he was looking at. When she saw it, her gaze shot to her mother.

"You left that picture in the scrapbook?"

"The Brandon picture," Lotty breathed, her eyes widening once more as it dawned on her. "We put it in that night and I forgot to take it out."

The photograph was an ordinary one like many of the others in the scrapbook of Cassie standing beside her homecoming or prom dates. Only the man she was standing next to in that last picture was not a man she wanted to see, and especially not one she wanted to have to explain.

"You look good," Joshua said as if that would make better the awkwardness that had suddenly developed. "You look happy...."

"Cassie was happy, but Brandon was a jerk," Reid said.

"Here, give me that picture," Luke added. "I'll get rid of it right now."

"It's okay," Cassie lied, wanting to crawl into a hole

yet again. "Let's not make a bigger deal out of it than it is," she suggested. Then to Joshua, she said, "It's an old picture of me and a guy I was with a while back. Just one of those things."

"We all have *those things* in our past," Joshua agreed, easing the tension by turning the page. But after that there were only blank pages, leaving that last picture still haunting them.

He closed the scrapbook and handed it back to Lotty, peering over the lazy Susan then and altering the tone that way. "Okay, where's the moose jerky? If no one else is going to try it, I guess I'll have to do it before we have dessert."

And again Cassie was grateful to him for how he handled the situation as her mother tried to discourage their guest from being the one to taste the jerky, and her brothers urged him on to what neither of them had agreed to do.

To Cassie's relief the remainder of the lunch went without incident as Joshua persuaded Luke and Reid and even her to taste the moose jerky that was salty, pungent, not altogether different than its beef counter-part. In fact, it was a good flavor to be followed by the ice cream and fruit that Lotty passed them each a bowl of afterward.

When dessert was finished, too, Lotty insisted the entire lunch mess be left for her to clean while everyone else went on with their day.

Because the meal had gone on longer than her allotted hour, Cassie accepted the offer and told everyone she'd see them that night. Once Joshua had said his own thanks and nice-to-meet-you-alls, he and Cassie went out the way they'd come in.

"Okay, so maybe lunch with the Walkers wasn't the best idea," Cassie said as she and Joshua walked back to the college campus.

Joshua laughed. "Probably not for you, but I had a great time."

"Uh-huh," she said dubiously, adding with a sarcastic note, "So great I'll bet you're dying to take us up on the invitation to Ben's open house tonight."

"As a matter of fact—"

"Come on, just be honest," Cassie said, cutting him off before he could make up an excuse. "I love my family and spending time with them, but after meeting them, the last thing you want to do is be with my mother and two *more* of my brothers tonight."

"As a matter of fact," Joshua repeated pointedly, "the guy whose house Alyssa went to last night was somebody she was interested in, and he is now just as interested in her. She tiptoed around it, but I have the distinct impression that she'd be more than happy for the chance to explore that mutual interest while it's in bloom. So when your mom invited me to your brother's party tonight, I was thinking that that might give me something to do that would free up Alyssa."

"Seriously?" Cassie said.

"Seriously," Joshua confirmed. "And also seriously, I don't know why you think I'd have a problem with your family or with meeting your other two brothers."

And she wasn't going to tell him why she thought that. Instead she said, "So you actually want to go tonight?"

"Sure," he said with a careless shrug. "Unless you don't want me to. I don't want to be a drag on you any more than I want to be a drag on my sister."

"No! I mean, you're not a drag on me and you really are welcome at the open house. I just thought this lunch was about enough for any one person to handle."

Joshua leaned to the side, butting her shoulder with his. "I'm sorry if *you* had a bad time, but I didn't. And unless you don't want me around tonight, I'd like to do that, too."

It would have been better if she *didn't* want him around tonight. Or any other time, Cassie thought.

But she did. In fact, suddenly her brother's open house had an entirely new appeal for her.

"Plus," Joshua added as they neared the building where her office was, "it'll look all the more like I'm here to see you, and it will keep some distance between Alyssa and me. People will be talking more about you and me than connecting me and my sister—exactly what we're after."

"Ah, so it isn't that you want to do my thing tonight, you just want to give Alyssa some space and keep up a good front," Cassie concluded.

"No, I want to give Alyssa some space and keep up a good front, *and* I want to do your thing tonight," he corrected.

Cassie didn't believe that but she didn't refute it again, either. She just nodded and said, "Okay. Sure."

They reached the front door of the administration building and paused there while she told him what time she'd pick him up. Her brother's facility was far enough outside of town that they'd have to drive there and she had no desire to get there on the back of his motorcycle.

Joshua pretended to be hurt by that but conceded before they said goodbye in time for him to find Alyssa between her classes.

As Cassie went inside she still didn't believe Joshua actually wanted to be with her—or her family—tonight. She was convinced that he was only pretending that was the case to give Alyssa some time to herself and himself something to do.

She didn't believe anything else because it seemed highly unlikely to her.

Yes, Ben's open house gave Joshua something to do while his sister was otherwise occupied and it kept up appearances to distract everyone from the truth of who he was.

But Cassie knew all too well that what he'd be doing and who he'd be doing it with couldn't possibly live up to his standards.

Even if he *did* know what pigs in a blanket were and had eaten every bit as many as each of her brothers.

Chapter Eight

"I want to take this opportunity to thank you all for coming and to thank the people who have helped make this happen."

Cassie's twin brother Ben was standing midway up the staircase in the entryway of the Northbridge School for Boys at eight o'clock Wednesday night, greeting the attendees of his open house. The large foyer was crowded with people. Most of the locals had come out in support of—or at least from curiosity about—the re-opening of the facility that would house and educate troubled adolescents.

Because of the number of people jammed into the area, Cassie was shoulder to broad shoulder with Joshua, who stood beside her as her brother listed each member of their family—her included—and what they'd done to aid in the remodeling, cleaning up, reorganizing, stocking and certifying of the placement home it had been Ben's goal to own and operate after his own troubled youth.

"I also want to bring Clair up here," Ben said, holding out a hand to encourage his fiancée to join him. "Most of you remember her and her father from when her father ran this place. And probably everybody knows by now that she and I will be married this Friday night and have a baby a few months from now—"

Laughter and applause accompanied a red-faced Clair's ascent to stand with Ben.

"I want to publicly thank Clair, too, for selling me the school in the first place, for her love and support, and for taking a chance on a former bad boy." Ben put his arm around Clair's shoulders and kissed her cheek. "I truly believe that together we're going to make this a great home for boys who need one. I'd also like—"

Ben had more to say but Cassie found it difficult to concentrate with Joshua so near.

She'd told him that this would be a dressy-jeans kind of occasion and tonight she'd forced herself not to overdo it. She was indeed wearing jeans—her best-fitting, vintage-washed pair that rode her hips like a lover's hand and just whispered across her rear end. To go with them, she'd chosen a pink sweater set that included a sleeveless turtleneck, fine-gauge sweater that looked classy and still hugged her body enough to be alluring, underneath a matching cardigan that hinted at that allure.

She'd also made sure to keep her makeup natural-looking, using only the amount of blush and mascara she would have under any circumstances.

It was just that Joshua looked *so* good that she couldn't help feeling as if she were nothing more than a pale shadow of the kind of woman he *could* have been with.

He had on jeans, too. Great jeans that cupped his terrific derriere as if they'd been made just for him— something she'd have guessed to be true except that they sported a common brand name on the leather tag at the waistband in back.

On top he was wearing a basket weave camel-colored knit shirt with a zip-mock collar that he'd left open, exposing the thick column of his neck and just brushing his sharp, cleanly shaven jawline. Over the shirt, he had on that leather jacket he'd worn the first night she'd met him, giving him a continental flare that made him look comfortable and elegant and sexy all at once.

Cassie was having trouble keeping her eyes off him. Even if it was surreptitious and only in sideways glances.

Why *did* the man have to look so amazing? she kept asking herself. Why couldn't he be some ham-faced mogul who was lucky to have money to get him girls, rather than a guy who could have been dirt-poor and still have had models flocking to him?

Ham-faced and paunchy, too, that would have made spending so much time with him less risky for her. Ham-faced, paunchy, arrogant and demanding—that would have helped even more.

But there he was, with a face too good to believe; a tall, muscular, well-built body and a personality that made him seem as down-home as any of her friends or acquaintances or coworkers or even her brothers.

I'm only human, she silently complained. *How am I supposed to be unaffected by all that?*

Then, as if in answer, the image of that last picture in her scrapbook came to mind.

No, Brandon hadn't been as handsome as Joshua. He hadn't had that kind of jaw-dropping, please-let-me-take-a-second-look body. But thinking about him, about how things had ended with him, about the differences between herself and Brandon and the illusion that those differences didn't matter? That was a pretty effective antidote.

You're not for me, Joshua Cantrell, she told herself. *And you never could be.*

"Again, thank you all for coming," Ben was saying. "Feel free to wander around, check the place out. There are drinks and some of Mom's best cookies and cakes in the dining room to help yourselves to, and please come to me with any concerns you might have about anything."

Ben's closing words penetrated Cassie's thoughts just before applause broke out around her.

"Concerns?" Joshua whispered, bending over to say it close enough to Cassie's ear for her to hear him. And close enough, too, for his breath to be warm and soft against her skin.

"This isn't a boarding school for rich kids," Cassie explained, refusing to think about how close he actually was to her. "It's a place parents and the courts send boys who have been in a whole lot of scrapes. Most of them will have prior arrest records and long histories of wreaking more than the average amount of havoc. They're kids in trouble, and not everyone in Northbridge has been thrilled to have them coming into town. There's been some worry voiced about troublemakers doing damage, vandalizing, starting fires, abusing animals, shoplifting, misbehaving— about anything the imagination can conjure has come up at one time or another."

"*Will* there be a danger?" Joshua asked.

Cassie knew he was concerned for his sister's safety even if he didn't say it outright. "No. Ben has installed more than ample security devices but this isn't a lockdown facility, so he won't accept boys with that kind of history. He also has a lot of other safeguards in place to prevent anything from happening that will disturb or affect the community in any way. Plus he has a zero-tolerance policy, which means that kids who step out of line won't be around to do it more than once."

"Sounds like a tough approach."

"That depends on how you look at it. Ben's philosophy was formed by his own experience as one of the kids who ended up in placement. He'll keep the boys busy with physical activities and chores to make sure they won't have the energy or the opportunity to get into mischief. On the other hand, it won't be anywhere near as harsh as the boot camp he went to. But believe me, the businesses and homeowners of Northbridge won't stand for having their safe, small-town life disrupted. If anything, I think Ben has more of a concern about letting his kids come into contact with the college kids and getting corrupted by what goes on at that level. I know he intends to keep a wide berth between the placement boys and the college, so you can relax when it comes to Alyssa and any of the kids who end up here."

Joshua still didn't admit or deny that was what had been on his mind. Instead, he seized on a different portion of what she'd said. "Ben was a troubled kid in placement himself?"

Most everyone else had filed out of the entryway, so Cassie and Joshua were alone there. But Cassie didn't have any desire to mingle—or to share Joshua—so she merely stayed put and answered his question about her twin.

"Ben was in a lot of trouble as a teenager. The straw that broke the camel's back was that he got picked up for stealing a car."

"I thought when I asked if my motorcycle would be safe Sunday night you said the only car theft in Northbridge was some old guy getting his own truck mixed up with someone else's."

"I believe what I said was that the *most recent* car theft was Ephram McCain's confusion. Before that, the only one was a car theft Ben and a friend of his were involved in. But Ben didn't actually steal a car. His friend told him it belonged to his friend's father and that the father had given them permission to drive it."

"But that wasn't the truth?"

"The car actually belonged to the friend's neighbor, and the friend had stolen it. But Ben was the one behind the wheel when the police pulled them over."

"So he was essentially innocent," Joshua concluded.

"Guilty of bad judgment and being dumb enough to believe that anyone would give a brand-new sports car to the two of them to joyride in. But innocent of car theft, yes. The problem was, Ben had been in so many messes before that that the judge and our mother decided it was time for some strong action to be taken. He was sent to a private facility in Arizona."

"Boot camp," Joshua repeated what she'd said about the place.

"Yes."

"And it was pretty bad, huh?"

"Bad but good. It was the turning point for Ben. Not only did he clean up his act, but he realized what he wanted to do with his life. That he wanted an education, that he wanted to work with kids like he was, and how he wanted to do that. It wasn't a nice time in his life—or for any of the family as we went through it with him—but so much positive came from the negative that it ended up being exactly what he needed."

Joshua's eyebrows arched towards his hairline. "Do you know what the tabloids would do with a story like that?"

Cassie couldn't help laughing. She made a point of glancing over her shoulder before she said, "There aren't a lot of those following the Walkers around."

"Right, but—"

"Besides, Ben's past isn't a secret. You heard him refer to himself as a bad boy. It's common knowledge around here. And his background, his philosophy and how he decided on the course of treatment for these kids is all in his brochure."

"I guess I was just thinking about my own situation and seeing headlines like: Former Delinquent Opens

School To Have His Own Private Band Of Miscreant Mercenaries For Mayhem In Small Montana Town."

"Long headline, but good alliteration," Cassie joked. "Are you sure you don't secretly write for one of those papers? Maybe that's why you show up on the covers so often."

"Believe me, no one would do to themselves what the tabloids have done to me," he said in all seriousness.

Apparently his notoriety was not a matter he always took as lightly as he'd claimed on Sunday night.

"There she is."

Cassie's conversation with Joshua was interrupted just then by the voice of yet another of her brothers. Looking in the direction of the recreation room, Cassie saw Ad and an entourage of his own approaching them.

"Mom sent us to find you. She said you have a surprise," Ad announced with a pointed gaze at Joshua.

Joshua extended his hand to Ad and then to the other man with Ad, and cashed in on being the *surprise* Lotty had mentioned. "Joshua Johansen," he introduced himself.

Wondering how long it was going to take her to get out from under the questions about why this pretend relationship hadn't turned into anything substantial, Cassie once again joined the charade to finish the introductions.

"Joshua, this is my brother Ad—he's the one who owns the restaurant. This is his wife, Kit. And this is Cutty Culhane and his wife Kira. Cutty has been friends with Ad forever and he's also part of the local police force with Luke."

Pleasantries were exchanged and then a ruminative Kit stared at Joshua and said, "You look familiar to me."

If that had happened before, Cassie hadn't been there to witness it and a sudden wave of panic washed through her.

Joshua, however, didn't show any signs of anxiety. "I get that a lot."

"He reminds me of someone, too, now that you mention it," Kira chimed in.

Joshua focused on Cassie. "What do you think? Do I look like someone else?"

Cassie tried to keep cool and shrugged. "You just look like Disneyland Guy to me."

"Disneyland Guy who you didn't tell anyone about," Ad chastised. "Ben and I both got slammed with calls from Mom, Luke and Reid this afternoon wanting to know if you'd told us about meeting a man on your vacation."

Cassie relaxed slightly to have successfully taken the focus off Joshua's appearance and said, "The lines at Disneyland were all long. I talked to a lot of people while I waited in them."

"I'm just the only one who actually tracked her down," Joshua chimed in.

"What he really did was take to heart my plug for the college for his sister," Cassie said before it occurred to her that connecting him with a sister he was that close to might spur something in either Kira's or Kit's minds. Then she panicked again and seized the only thing she could think of to get them away from the situation. "So what did Mom make for refreshments for tonight?" she asked too eagerly.

Luckily that seemed to succeed. Both women recited

a list of the foods set out buffet-style in the other room, and, after claiming to be hungry, Cassie suggested she and Joshua get something to eat.

"Thanks for the help back there," Joshua said when they were well out of earshot of Ad, his wife and his friends.

"Just doing my job," Cassie responded.

Throughout the remainder of the evening, no one else seemed to have any suspicions that Joshua wasn't who he was introduced as. But still, Cassie was relieved when the open house ended and she and Joshua said good-night to her family and finally left.

"So. Is that true?" Joshua said as Cassie drove down the long drive that led away from the Northbridge School For Boys.

Since they hadn't been talking about anything at all, a confused Cassie took her eyes off the road for a moment to glance at him. "Is what true?"

"Earlier, I thanked you for the support when your brother's wife and her friend thought they recognized me. You said you were just doing your job. Is that true? Is that the *only* reason you're hanging out with me?"

"That's the *only* reason you're hanging out with me," she countered rather than answer a question that didn't have a simple, cut-and-dried answer for her.

"It might be the only reason I got to meet you, but I don't know about the rest," he said.

Cassie gave him a wry look. "Like I believe that," she said, thinking he was merely showing her a little of the charm that had won him legions of other women.

Joshua laughed. "You're calling me a liar?"

"A player is more like it."

"Then you *do* read the tabloids and buy into what they say."

"The headlines are enough. But I suppose in reality you're a monk," Cassie said facetiously.

"In reality I haven't even *met* half the women they show me with in their doctored pictures. And while no, I'm not a monk, I'm not a player, either."

Something about the way he said that—without any defensiveness, just as if it were a fact—made it actually seem possible.

"Okay, you're not a player or a monk," she conceded as she headed around the campus to the rear where the chancellor's cottage was. "But you still wouldn't be hanging out with me if I wasn't assigned to you."

"I wouldn't have *met* you," he reiterated. "I would have been *assigned* to someone else and that someone else would have only steered me toward things that would impress upon me that the college could use donations—"

And the town, Cassie thought, but didn't add.

"Which means that I probably wouldn't have had the opportunity to meet you," Joshua continued. "But if I had…"

"If you had," Cassie finished for him, not letting that innuendo-laden ending go, "you would have barely given me the time of day and gone on about your business without giving me a second thought."

"Wrong."

"Not wrong," she insisted.

"Wrong," he insisted more firmly. "With dimples like yours? I'd have definitely made some inquiries."

She honestly thought he was just making flattering small talk. But it was fun, so she went along with it. "Inquiries are not the same as hanging out with me."

"Inquiries would only have been the beginning."

"Uh-huh," Cassie said dubiously. "And what would have followed?"

"Maybe a ride on my motorcycle if you weren't all afraid and prim and proper and girly."

Cassie laughed. "That is *sooo* transparent."

"What?"

"Trying to play on the fact that I was raised with four brothers and didn't get away with being too *girly.* You think that by accusing me of it, you will goad me into getting on that thing."

She glanced at him again and found him grinning before he said, "Dimples, and the fact that I can never get one over on you—that's why I'd hang out with you even if you weren't being forced to hang out with me."

"I'm not being *forced,*" she finally admitted, although quietly, reluctantly, and knowing she shouldn't. "Especially not when it comes to things like tonight, which was a family thing, if you'll recall."

"A family thing *you* didn't invite me to, your mother did. Which means you wouldn't have been hanging out with me there tonight if not for her because it wasn't part of the job description."

"I invited you to my mother's house for lunch today," Cassie said, sounding as defensive as he'd managed not to earlier.

"Only after I hinted around at it. It was more like I invited myself to lunch today. Proving that I would have hung out with you, but you wouldn't have hung out with me."

Cassie pulled up to the curb near the path that led to the rear of the chancellor's cottage. "I'm not going to win this, am I?" she said when she'd brought the car to a stop.

"No," Joshua said, clearly enjoying his victory. "Or, on the other hand…" he added as if something had just occurred to him "…you could show me I'm completely off base and go for a ride on my motorcycle."

Cassie laughed again. "If coming at something one way doesn't work, you just come at it another way?"

"Points for persistence. Now what do you say? The night is young and warm, and you're not in show-the-world-you're-a-professional clothes for once, and I found an interesting place not far out of town."

"You want to go motorcycle riding now?"

"Right now. Moonlight motorcycle riding. Come on, I'll have you back in an hour."

He probably *was* a player, Cassie thought, because he was just too appealing, too charismatic, too alluring for her to refuse, and probably for any other woman to refuse, either.

But there was also the fact that if she *did* refuse, she would be putting an end to this time with him. And now that that moment was upon her, she didn't really want to.

"Are you a safe driver?" she challenged.

"You can wear my helmet and I'll go five miles under the speed limit if it makes you feel better," he promised.

"No helmets," she said, making a face at that idea and thinking more about her hair than her safety.

"Okay, I'll go ten miles under the speed limit. But then I want an hour and a half."

"Negotiations?" she said with another smile.

"Yep."

"Okay. But if my brother Reid knew I was on the back of a motorcycle without a helmet—at any speed— he'd kill me."

"I won't tell if you won't."

Chapter Nine

Cassie's first motorcycle ride taught her a few things. It taught her that she liked the sense of freedom, the open air, the vibration and even the loud roar of the engine as Joshua drove through the quiet, deserted country roads outside of Northbridge.

It taught her that helmet or no helmet, there was no escaping hair gone wild.

And it taught her that when she was fighting an attraction to a man, the last thing she should do was ride a motorcycle with him.

Sitting close behind Joshua, she caught intermittent whiffs of a clean, citrusy cologne in the clear breeze. Her legs straddled his hips, her arms were wrapped around him, and her breasts brushed against his expansive back. It was like craving chocolate and having an entire banquet of the stuff set out before her but not being allowed a single taste. It was a situation to avoid, not a situation to embrace.

But realizing that and making a mental note for future reference didn't alter the fact that the heat of his body was warming her and she would very much have liked to press herself completely against him, to lie her cheek to the side of his neck, and really make a night of it.

She just didn't give in to the inclination.

When he pulled off the main road onto a much narrower one that was more a path through a densely wooded area, Cassie knew exactly where he was headed. She just didn't know why he was headed there. But at least she was forewarned so she could remind herself not to get carried away, so she could shore up her defenses against what was already bubbling up inside of her.

Then they reached the clearing that brought the old north bridge into sight and when Joshua had come to within several yards of it, he stopped the motorcycle and turned off the engine.

"Alyssa and I found this today and wondered about it," he said over his shoulder. "I thought this might be a good spot for a little stargazing. Or are you cold?"

She'd had a wool peacoat in her car and had put it on over the sweater set, and since the temperature hadn't dropped as precipitously yet as it did most evenings, she thought she could weather being out a little longer. "I'm okay."

"Good," he said.

Joshua had zipped up the neck of his shirt and his

leather jacket, too, and was obviously warm enough, as well, because he got off the motorcycle and turned to help Cassie off as he continued with the subject of the bridge.

"At first when Alyssa and I spotted it, we thought we'd found some old deserted relic, but then we got close enough to see that something was being done to it."

"It's Northbridge's namesake," Cassie said as she pretended not to notice his outstretched hand and swung a leg over the seat on her own.

"But it's south of town," Joshua pointed out.

"And north of the farms and ranches that were here before there *was* a town. Which was why it was referred to as the *north* bridge. Then the town was built, named after the bridge and I guess no one was supposed to notice that the north bridge was to the south of North-bridge."

"Believe it or not, I understood that," Joshua said with a laugh. "We could see it better in the daylight this afternoon, but it looks like it's getting a face-lift."

"It's being restored," Cassie confirmed, aiming her own gaze in the direction of the bridge.

Only moonlight broke the darkness but there was enough of it to illuminate the work that had begun on the covered bridge that spanned what had once been a river but was now just an ambling stream. There were gaps in the crosshatch bars that ran along the top of the solid lower-half sides, and there were also temporary supports replacing some of the posts that held the roof that was awaiting repair and new shingles.

"We're turning this area into a park with the bridge as

the focal point," she continued. "Sort of a historic site, I guess you could say. It should be nice when it's finished."

"Alyssa and I thought it was nice out here even today. Quiet. Peaceful. How 'bout we sit on the creek bank for a while?"

"Maybe just for a little while," Cassie agreed.

The creek bank was steep enough to form a grassy ledge and that was where Cassie went to sit, even though it put the stream into view more than the stars.

But Joshua didn't complain. He merely joined her there, sitting close enough for her to continue to feel the heat of his body along her side now without actually touching her.

Which was not something Cassie wanted to think about so she sought refuge in more details of the bridge's reconstruction.

When she'd exhausted that topic, Joshua leaned back enough to brace his weight on his hands. Cassie felt a distinctive cooling and was sorry he'd put any distance between them, even though she knew that, for the sake of resisting what the nearness of the man could do to her, the more distance the better.

"You must be on the rebuild-the-bridge committee to know so much about it," he said then.

"No, but I do go to the town meetings where we're kept informed."

"So your job doesn't *always* keep you busy night and day."

"This would be the first time."

She could feel him studying her profile but refused to look at him.

"And how did you come to this job that's brought you and I together?" he asked.

"No special way. I graduated with a bachelor's degree in education and one in psychology—"

"A double major? I'm impressed."

"And then I got my master's in educational counseling. Which isn't what my formal title is, but when the freshman adviser's position opened, I was just graduating and needed the job."

"Which involves more advice on what classes to take than on how to mend broken hearts?"

"Yes. But since we don't have a school psychologist on staff, whenever students have an emotional issue or problem, they get sent to me, too."

"The small town wearing-of-many-hats?"

"Exactly."

Cassie did finally glance at him, turning to do it somewhat over her shoulder because of the way he was sitting. "Now you," she said.

"Now me?"

"You told me at the bonfire that you went to work for the same company your father worked for, a company that made and sold ladies' high heels."

"Right."

"I've been wondering since then how you went from that to being the Tennis Shoe Tycoon."

"Ah. It wasn't a huge leap. I think I also told you that I started at the manufacturing end—"

"You did," she said, wanting him to know he wasn't the only one of them to pay attention.

"Well, I basically learned the business from the

ground up." He chuckled slightly. "*Huge leap, ground up*—I'm just full of shoe puns tonight. Although it's the truth—I did learn about good soles, good heels, the stuff that touches the ground, and then I moved into shoes that got marketed for their ability to help in jumping high, so I guess it all applies. Anyway, literally and figuratively, I learned from the ground up—shoe manufacturing, handling, selling, distributing, the whole nine yards."

"When it came to ladies' shoes," Cassie reminded.

"Right. But believe it or not, ladies' shoes didn't hold a lot of interest for me."

"Really?" Cassie said with a voice full of innuendo.

He caught it and laughed, a sound that was deep and rich and somehow made her feel very accomplished to have caused it.

"Okay, when there is someone *in* ladies' shoes, then what they're holding is something of great interest to me. But the shoes themselves—not so much. Still, it became a business I knew and so I plugged in something else I was interested in—sports of all kinds—and I came up with my own tennis shoe design, based mainly on what I wanted most in a shoe—performance, durability, comfort and style."

"And it took off for you just that easily?"

"No, there were a few missteps—"Again he chuckled. "I just can't stop this tonight."

"Uh-huh."

"Anyway, my first two designs were bad. But I had a friend who was in medical school and I got him to talk to me about the human foot, about weight distribution, balance, orthopedics, things like that, and I incorporated it all in my third design. That one showed promise and so Alyssa and I went out on a limb."

"How did you do that?"

"What little there was of the insurance money from the folks' death—I'd been tapping into it only out of necessity and in emergencies—Alyssa and I decided to invest in a company of our own."

"Alyssa was how old when she helped make that decision?" Cassie asked with another glance at Joshua.

"She was eleven," he said. "I know, hardly an advanced age for an objective decision. But honestly, I was worried enough about doing it that if she'd said no, I wouldn't have done it."

"But she didn't say no?"

"She was actually very mature about it all. She listened to everything I had to say. Checked out the prototype for the shoes. She even asked enough questions to let me know she was aware that if the venture didn't work out, we were going to be in even worse financial trouble than we already were—barely making ends meet on the money I made working for Dad's old company. But ultimately she liked the shoes—if only I'd put pink or yellow or baby-blue stripes on some of them so girls could wear them, too, she said—and finally she told me to go for it. She even offered to get a paper route and start babysitting if I failed."

"So you did it."

"So *we* did it. Alyssa is an equal partner—that seemed only fair since half the insurance money was hers."

That wasn't something Cassie had known before. "I've always heard that the company is yours."

"Tabloids again. They always leave out the truth. And the truth is that Alyssa and I share fifty-fifty."

"But you do all the work?"

"For now. I'm thinking that eventually she'll come into that, too."

Cassie looked at him a third time, trying not to let it register how ruggedly handsome were the stark lines and shadows of his face in the moon's glow. "Okay, then how did you go from taking a huge risk with the only money you and your sister had to being the darling of the media?"

"The darling of the media?" he repeated disdainfully, obviously not thrilled with that title.

"That's what you are, isn't it? One of them, anyway. Hounded by photographers, written about in newspapers and magazines—and all for *sneakers?*"

"Hey! They're great shoes," he defended as if she'd insulted them. But he hadn't taken offense because he sat up straight again and smiled at her. "Being a *media darling* was never my goal. Or even a thought in my head that it would happen or was possible. It was accidental. Or co-incidental. Or both, maybe. First the shoes took off—"

"Quit with the puns," Cassie jokingly reprimanded.

"Well, they did. They were a hit. A couple of people training for track and field in the Olympics were wearing them, a tennis ace, a basketball superstar—basically a lot of professional athletes. I got some of them to agree to endorse the shoes, became friendly with a few and ended up with courtside tickets to some big deal events. Courtside meant I'd just happen to be sitting among celebrities—who were also beginning to wear my shoes. The media tracked the celebrities and my face would show up here and there in the corner of one of their pictures just because I was in the same general area—"

"Famous by proximity?"

"Pretty much. One night, a photographer spotted me on the way out of a basketball game and said, *'Who are you, anyway? Are you somebody?'*"

"Nice," Cassie commented, interpreting the mimicked tone of voice Joshua had used for the quote.

"Some of them are, but this guy was one of the jerks. Still, I told him who I was, figuring I might get a little free publicity for the shoes. It never occurred to me that it would go anywhere from there."

"Only it did."

"The next thing I knew, I was splashed over magazines and newspapers as some kind of boy wonder. My net worth became public knowledge, and pictures of me that I didn't even know had been taken were showing up everywhere I looked. All of a sudden, where I'd been or who I'd been with started to become news. To tell you the truth, I've never understood how it came to this or why anybody would care or actually buy papers or magazines to read about what I'm doing."

Cassie understood it. She only had to look at him again to know the reason behind it—besides that, he'd become a megamillionaire before he was twenty-five. He had a jaw-droppingly gorgeous face and the body to go with it. A jaw-droppingly gorgeous face and body that photographed well. Women seeing it even just in the background of a picture of someone else would want to know who he was. And the media had obliged, latched on to him and never let go.

An unexpected shiver shook Cassie just then and while she wasn't sure whether it was from the rapidly cooling evening air or from just looking at Joshua, he attributed it to the chill.

"I better take you back," he said, wasting no time standing.

When he held his hand out to help her up, she couldn't very well ignore it again and had to accept it. But as with every contact with him, no matter how small, it roused things in Cassie that lingered long after she was on her feet and he'd let go of her hand.

Maybe because of that lingering titillation, the return trip to the college sitting behind him on the motorcycle seemed shorter than the trip out had been. But all too soon—for Cassie, at any rate—Joshua was parking the Harley-Davidson a few feet to the rear of her sedan where it waited at the curb of the street near the chancellor's cottage.

"There you go—back in one piece. Safe and sound," Joshua announced into the silence left when he turned off the engine. As he settled the motorcycle onto its stand he said, "What did you think of your first ride?"

"I liked it," she confessed, hooking her hair around her ears and sweeping her bangs out of her eyes in hopes of doing some damage control.

Once more he got off the bike first and turned to offer

her help, and before Cassie had considered whether or not she should accept it, she saw her hand slide into his.

Only this time, even after both of her feet were firmly on the pavement, he didn't let go. He went on holding her hand as he walked her to the driver's side of her car.

"Tomorrow is the day I play college student and go with Alyssa to abbreviated versions of all her classes," Joshua informed Cassie along the way. "But the dinner at the mayor's house that is apparently in my honor in the evening would bore her to death, so I told her she didn't have to come. I've been informed, though, that you'll be my escort...."

Cassie had been informed of that, too, late that afternoon when the dean had appeared in her office to announce to her that the mayor would be throwing a small, discreet dinner party for Joshua and that she was to be in attendance.

"More work-related command performance?" Joshua guessed.

"Maybe the mayor has just decided to add me to his usual guest list," Cassie answered glibly.

But she didn't fool Joshua. As they came to a stop at her car door, he said, "You don't have to do it."

Cassie didn't open the door or get in. Instead she merely turned her back to it and leaned her hips there. Primarily because she didn't want to lose Joshua's hand wrapped so warmly, so familiarly around hers just yet.

"I heard your mom talking about Ben's rehearsal dinner tomorrow night," Joshua continued. "I'm sure you need to be—and would rather be—at that."

Which was what she'd told the dean. It just hadn't

gotten her anywhere when he'd called the mayor from her desk phone and told the mayor that. The mayor had demanded to speak to her to further impress upon her her civic responsibilities, reminding her that Ad's liquor license was up for renewal in a few months and what a shame it would be if it didn't get the okay.

"It's all right," she said. "I don't need to rehearse. And I'll have dinner at the mayor's house, so I'll still be fed," she added, trying to make light of it and not let Joshua know she'd been blackmailed into being his dinner partner.

"You really are a dedicated employee and a true and worthy daughter of Northbridge," he said wryly.

In that instant Cassie discovered that she didn't want Joshua thinking that the only reason she would be with him was because someone else was pushing her to be. Although she wasn't exactly sure why it made any difference to her when he clearly already knew the score.

"Didn't I just prove I wasn't being forced to hang out with you by riding that motorcycle?" she countered.

"For tonight, maybe," he said, his dark hair nearly blue-black in the light that fell on them from the street lamp nearby and his silver-gray eyes still gleaming as they peered into hers. "But tomorrow night? Going to some hokey dinner at the mayor's house instead of to the rehearsal dinner for your brother's wedding? I don't believe that anything short of force could make you do that."

"Then, too," she added facetiously, "you *are* such an awful person that anyone would have to have his or her arm twisted to be with you. If that weren't the case, you could even come to the rehearsal dinner."

"Could I come to the rehearsal as your date or just as your tagalong again?" he asked hypothetically in a voice that was deep, quiet, intimate and teasingly inquisitive all at once.

"You could come as my date," Cassie decreed as if she'd be doing him a favor.

He raised their entwined hands and said, "A date who could hold your hand even with your family around to see it?"

"Maybe," she said, still maintaining the less serious note.

Or was she flirting with him?

Joshua took a step closer, standing very near to her, facing her. "A date who could kiss you good night when he brought you home afterward?"

"Like last night?" she said, raising an eyebrow at him as if that kiss had been of questionable value.

"Well, if last night didn't do it for you then I guess not. But maybe I could try again…"

He leaned forward and pressed his lips to hers, softly, gingerly at first, the way he'd kissed her the second time the night before, only long enough tonight for her to kiss him back, to enjoy the feel of his mouth on hers, before he ended it.

In keeping with the game they were playing about whether or not he could be the kind of date who could kiss her good-night like that, she said, "Yeah, that's pretty safe."

Joshua mock frowned down at her. "*Safe?* Just what I want to be known as—the *safe* kisser."

"What kind of kisser do you want to be known as?"

Oh yeah, she was flirting all right. She was definitely flirting. And playing with fire...

Joshua smiled the devil's own smile and used the hand he still held to pull her to him this time, wrapping his other arm around her to keep her tightly up against him as his mouth found hers again, forcefully but in a way that was purely sexy.

Forcefully and sexily enough to sweep her off her feet as his lips parted and persuaded hers to part, too. As his tongue introduced itself, urging her lips to open wider, to let him in, to find hers and tempt it out of timidity.

And before she knew it, he'd released her hand and put that arm around her to bring her up against him.

Before she knew it, her arms were around him, too. Her hands were splayed against his broad, muscular back. Her nipples were hard little knots nudging at his chest. And her tongue was meeting his, matching his, giving as good as she got.

And what she was getting *was* good! So good!

She'd never felt anything quite as good as being held there in those particular big, strong arms. She'd never felt anything quite as good as having her body melded to his. She'd never felt anything quite as good as his mouth over hers, willing to lead and to follow, to explore and be explored, to tempt and tease and entice, and then appease and please and start over again.

She'd just plain never felt anything as good as that connection with him, that contact, that moment with that man when mouths were open wide and tongues were plundering freely and this felt like only the beginning...

Until one tiny thought broke free and reminded her

that that man was Joshua Cantrell. That that man was a man out of reach to her in a greater sense than in that moment she was having with him.

That that man was not the man for her …

Cassie eased into ending the kiss, struggling to make herself stop something that she just wanted to go on and on and on.

But she did it anyway. She withdrew by slow measures, until the kiss was over and she'd dropped her forehead to his chest while she worked to maintain the resolve that had reminded her of the reality of this situation.

"Damn. If you say that was just part of the job, too, I'm going to be crushed," Joshua said in a husky whisper above her.

Cassie could only shake her head, almost as if she were boring a hole into him, denying that her job, her loyalty to Northbridge, that anything outside of her own attraction to him had been responsible for what she'd just allowed to happen between them.

Joshua kissed her crown and then stayed with his nose in the same spot, breathing hot air into her hair. "As much as I'd like to cash in on whatever pressure you're under to keep me company," he said, abandoning the teasing tone they'd been engaged in before, "I mean it— go to your brother's wedding rehearsal tomorrow night. I know what's on the agenda for things like the mayor's dinner. The mayor will pretend he's just being friendly then work it into the conversation that I should consider Northbridge as the site of a new shoe factory, or a distri- bution center, or as the best place to launch a hotel empire or whatever else is on his mind. You shouldn't miss a special occasion with your family just to round out the head count at the dinner table for something like that."

Except that Ad's liquor license was riding on it, Cassie told herself.

"I already said I would come. It's okay. Really," she assured.

Joshua raised his head from hers and she followed suit to look him in the eye again, finding him smiling a small smile at her.

"Is this something I'm going to have to feel guilty about?" he asked.

"Yes," she said emphatically, just because she knew he wasn't expecting it.

Joshua laughed. "It might be worth it to have you there to break up the boredom."

He kissed her again, a slow, leisurely kiss that kept tongues in check but still managed to send tiny shock waves through Cassie before it was over. Then he took his arms from around her to grasp her shoulders in his hands, holding her in place while he stepped one step backward.

"I suppose you also have orders to pick me up and take me to the mayor's house," Joshua guessed.

She did and she didn't deny that, either. She merely said, "Seven o'clock sharp."

"Honestly, you don't have to do it."

She did, though. She just didn't want him thinking that. "I know I don't *have* to. But I'm going to."

His smile this time was pleased. "I'll make it up to you. Just tell me how. Anything you want."

"A whole trunk full of diamonds and rubies, nothing less," Cassie joked.

"I'll get my people right on it," he assured, leaving her wondering if he actually had *people* to set to tasks, and thinking that he probably did.

Then, on the off chance that he hadn't realized she was kidding, she said, "On second thought, skip the diamonds and rubies and just listen to whatever it is the mayor has to say." But not because she had any idea what that might be or that it could be worthwhile to Joshua, just because she suddenly had the image of him actually investing in Northbridge and possibly having a reason to come back…

"You drive a hard bargain," he said, pretending to concede only against his will.

He let go of her arms then and got out of the way of her moving enough to open the door.

"Have fun in class tomorrow," she said as she finally got behind the steering wheel.

"Maybe I'll act as if I'm in crisis and get myself sent to your office," he said as he pushed the door to within an inch of closing, peering down at her from above the window.

"Uh-huh," she said dubiously. "But in case that doesn't work out, I'll see you at seven tomorrow night."

"Seven. Tomorrow night," he repeated as if it were important to him.

Then he closed her door and stepped into the middle of the street so she could pull away from the curb.

But as she did Cassie kept her eye more on her rearview mirror than on the road, watching Joshua watch her drive off.

And she knew that even though on the surface she

was bypassing Ben's wedding rehearsal and dinner so that Ad's liquor license wouldn't be in any jeopardy, all the mayor had actually done with that threat was give her the excuse.

Because despite the fact that her family was the focal point of her life, despite the fact that her twin brother was getting married and she would miss the first leg of the celebration for that, she still didn't feel any regret.

What she felt was Joshua's mouth on hers as surely as if it were there yet.

What she felt was all atingle inside.

What she felt was a hope that the rest of the night and the next day would pass as quickly as that motorcycle ride home had seemed to.

And even though she told herself she had to be out of her mind to be doing and feeling every bit of it, that was how it was.

She was thrilled to death to know as she lost sight of Joshua that it was a sure thing that she'd be seeing him again the next night.

At any cost.

Chapter Ten

"Hey, what's up with you? I haven't been able to get three words in a row out of you all day."

Joshua had finally reached the end of his patience with his sister by late the next afternoon. They'd finished with the day's dash through each of the classes on her schedule and were back at the chancellor's cottage. Joshua had suggested going for coffee or ice cream or a walk in the town square but had been met with only uninterested shrugs in answer to each one. After a day full of those kinds of responses, he'd given up, brought Alyssa to the privacy of the cottage and decided to address what he'd originally thought was PMS or a generic bad mood but was now thinking otherwise.

"Are you PO'd at me for something?" he added.

"You said you wouldn't do it," Alyssa said, clearly unhappy with him.

"I said I wouldn't do what?"

"Get into anything with Cassie Walker. But last night, Tim walked me back to the dorm and we took the long way around and I saw the two of you."

There was enough righteous indignation in his sister's tone to let Joshua know that Alyssa had to have seen him kissing Cassie at her car after their motorcycle ride.

Alyssa had come into the cottage and plopped down on the sofa. Joshua had remained standing. But now he sat, too, in the armchair directly across from the couch and his sister.

"Yeah, okay, I kissed her," he admitted guiltily. "I know I shouldn't have. I knew I shouldn't be doing it when I did it."

"But you did it anyway. A hot one."

Great, she'd seen it all….

"Too hot to be a first kiss," Alyssa continued. "You said you wouldn't do this with her and there you were. Tim didn't know it was you at first, he just saw the two of you there, like that, and he said, 'Get a room'—that's how hot it was."

"It wasn't *that* bad," Joshua defended feebly.

"You shouldn't have been kissing her at all. You said you wouldn't do this and you did."

Joshua sighed and gave up trying to defend the indefensible. "I know," he said. "I'm sorry. I just… I like her."

"You liked her from the start. But we talked about this, about her being the same kind of person as Jennie, only more so, and how that made her wrong for you and you promised you wouldn't go after her."

"I know, I know."

"So what did you do, forget? About Jennie and all that? Did you forget what happened? What could happen again?"

"No, I didn't forget. But…I don't know, I guess being here is like being almost on another planet—somewhere where things are different. So far, we're fitting in and we've had the chance to be like everyone else and it all feels safe and removed, and… I don't know," he repeated. "It's just been nice. Nice not having to look over my shoulder. Nice to just be myself. Nice to just get to know Cassie and her family…" He took a deep breath and sighed it out with a shrug before he concluded, "It's just been nice."

"I know," Alyssa said. "It *is* nice here and it's nice to fit in. But even if I get away with being here to go to school and live for a while in peace, you know you aren't going to be able to hide here forever."

If only…

"I know," he conceded.

"But now you have something going on with Cassie."

"I like her," he repeated.

"Too bad you don't like her enough to protect her."

"Low blow," Joshua shot back at his sister, frowning at her.

"It's true, isn't it? If you *really* liked her, you'd want to spare her."

He shook his head. "That isn't true at all. *Really* liking her is the trouble. And *really* liking her here is double the trouble. When I'm with her, I'm just with her—it's as if nothing else exists, as if I don't have any other life away from that, as if… I don't know, as if I'm in this little isolation booth because looking at her, listening to her, being with her, tunes everything else out. Everything else recedes and gets very small and insignificant, and it's just her and me, and I'm having such a good time I don't want there to be anything else. Plus we're in Northbridge—no one is recognizing me, people are taking me at face value, and I suppose that's made it all the easier to feel as if I've escaped, as if I'm free to actually do this and be with her and let down my guard and enjoy myself."

"I'm sorry."

That reaction and the heartfelt sympathy in it sounded so contradictory to what he'd just said that it made Joshua laugh. "Yeah, me, too. Sorry I *can't* hide out here forever."

"And have Cassie."

There was a part of him that was screaming that maybe he *could* still have Cassie, even after the reality of his life invaded. But Alyssa and her angry reminder of his past didn't allow him to hang on to that for long.

Still, war waged within him and he said, "Cassie *is* something, you know? She's smart and funny and quick. And she has those incredible turquoise eyes and those dimples, and damn, but I have a good time when I'm with her."

"So I saw last night."

"It's not just that, though, Alyssa. Not just the physical stuff—"

Although there was a whole lot of the physical stuff, the physical attraction that had sent him to bed with images of Cassie in his head every night since he'd met her.

The physical attraction that had him wishing she was with him whenever she wasn't—particularly in that bed.

The physical attraction that had him thinking about her face, her hair, her body even when he was on the phone talking tennis shoes.

The physical attraction that had him wondering every time he knew he was about to see her again if there would be any opportunity for him to touch her or get her alone or kiss her. Wondering how far he could go if he *did* get to kiss her. Savoring each second of those kisses he had stolen and then reliving them in his mind, keeping the memory of every detail vividly alive, the memory of getting her into his arms, of holding her, of his hands in her hair or on her back, of having her pressed to him, her breasts against his chest…

Yeah, there was a whole lot of the physical stuff. A whole lot more of the physical stuff that he wanted to happen, that went far beyond just kissing her…

But he wasn't going to tell his little sister that.

Instead he said, "Okay, sure, there's some physical stuff, but there's also more to it than that with Cassie. There's—"

"There's what there was with Jennie."

Only even more…

More already in the feelings that were coming up for Cassie.

But he couldn't tell Alyssa that, either.

"I didn't choose it," he said.

"I know, it's chemistry. But you still have to fight it," Alyssa decreed pragmatically.

If only it were that easy...

"Believe it or not, I'm trying," Joshua said. And it was the truth. He just wasn't succeeding.

"Yeah, it looked like you were trying real hard last night," Alyssa countered.

"Come on, cut me a little slack here. I'm only human."

"But so is she. And do you think she could take what Jennie went through any better than Jennie did?"

"No."

"Then do you really want to do that to her?"

Or to Alyssa—Joshua knew that was the unspoken addition to the reminder his sister was giving him.

"No," he repeated.

"So don't."

Simple as that.

Too bad it *wasn't* as simple as that.

"It's not like I'm not fighting it, Alyssa. I am. I really, really am."

"Maybe you're fighting it when you're *not* with her. But when you are? You're in that isolation booth and you don't fight, you give in anyway," Alyssa summarized, proving she knew him all too well.

Joshua shrugged, not seeing the point in arguing the truth. "Still, I *am* trying."

"Well, try harder."

"You want to write that on my hand, see if that helps?" he joked.

"Just keep your hands to yourself," Alyssa ordered. "And your lips, too."

"Oh, sure, I have to behave, but I'll bet you got a good-night kiss last night, didn't you?" Joshua countered.

Alyssa smiled beatifically. "Yes, I did. A good one, too."

"I'd think that might inspire a little sympathy for me and what you're telling me to cut out."

"I just don't want to have to feel sorrier for Cassie later on," Alyssa said.

"Yeah, neither do I," Joshua agreed.

The problem was, what he was feeling for Cassie now didn't have anything to do with sorrow or sympathy. And what he was feeling for Cassie now was growing at such a rapid rate, to such intense levels, that it was virtually impossible to simply turn it off because he *didn't* want to be sorry later on.

But since all Alyssa knew was that he'd agreed with her point of view, she seemed to be willing to end the conversation and grant him amnesty by announcing that they should have sodas.

As she got up to get them, Joshua sank back into the armchair and lectured himself about the wisdom in his younger sister's concerns and cautions and alarms, and about the lack of wisdom in his own actions.

Especially when he recalled some of the things he'd already learned about Cassie and about the people who meant the most to her.

So he truly needed to back off when it came to her, he told himself. He needed to back *way* off and not let what he was feeling or any amount of any kind of attraction to her rule.

And he wanted to. He honestly did. Because what

he *didn't* want was for anything bad to happen to Cassie or to anyone she cared about because of an association with him.

It was just that being with her *did* give him the sense that they were removed, that they were free, that nothing could possibly go wrong.

And when he was in that frame of mind, in that isolation booth with Cassie, the only thing that mattered was that moment he was getting to have with her. The attraction to her. The chemistry between them. The connection he felt with her.

The connection he felt with her that he just wanted to let get stronger and stronger.

"I'm sorry, Mayor McCullum, but I'm going to have to cut this short."

Cassie glanced at Joshua where he sat beside her on the mayor's sofa, surprised by the way he suddenly looked and sounded. When she'd walked out her front door this evening to pick him up she'd discovered him waiting for her outside.

The overcast sky had brought with it a chilly wind, and Joshua had been leaning his hips against the rear fender of her car, his arms folded over his chest, his legs crossed at the ankles. He was dressed in a black cashmere turtleneck sweater, black wool slacks and a long black coat that had all worked together to stop her in her tracks the minute she caught sight of him. Cosmopolitan. Fabulous. Outrageously sexy. And certainly robustly healthy.

But as she glanced at him now, his brows were beetled and his expression made it appear that he was in pain.

"I get miserable migraine headaches out of the blue," he said then. "And I'm afraid I'm getting one right now."

"What can I get you?" the mayor demanded. "A doctor? Cassie's brother is a doctor. We'll have him over here in five minutes, won't we, Cassie?"

If the mayor and his dinner commandeered another Walker from Ben's rehearsal tonight, Cassie thought her mother might storm the mayor's house.

But before she could say anything at all, Joshua said, "I've seen doctors. There's very little they can do for me. I have pills back at the chancellor's cottage and taking those and sleeping it off are the only things that will get me through it. Which means I'm going to have to beg off dinner before it even gets started."

"Oh, no—"

"Like I said, I'm sorry, but there's nothing else I can do. Let me just tell you, though, that I like it here in Northbridge and so does my sister. And if you can help keep the fact that she's here out of the press so she can have four peaceful years, I'll be forever in your debt. I guarantee that I'll make it worthwhile for this town and for the college in whatever way I can."

"Wonderful!" the mayor said, excited and instantly losing his concern for Joshua's health. "I assure you that everything that can possibly be done to protect the privacy of you and of your sister will be done."

"That's what I like to hear. I'll make sure to call your office before I leave town and we can have a chat about where I might be best able to make Alyssa's stay here of benefit to Northbridge. But for now, I just have to say good night and have Cassie drive me back."

"Of course. Get him right home, Cassie," the mayor decreed.

"I will," Cassie said as everyone in the room—Cassie, Joshua, the mayor, the mayor's wife, most of the college's administrative board and the members of the town council—stood.

"Please, go on with your cocktails. I'm sure Cassie knows the way out," Joshua insisted.

"At least allow me to walk with you," the mayor said.

The distance to the front door wasn't far, but even so the mayor managed to mention the reconstruction of the bridge and how funding would help considerably, as well as several other ideas he had that he thought Joshua might be interested in.

"We'll talk," Joshua said in answer to it all as Cassie retrieved his coat from the hall tree, handed it to him and then got her own.

Joshua had his coat on by the time she had hers in hand and he took it from her, holding it for her to slip into.

Cassie had opted for a fitted long-sleeved rose-colored, square-neck lace top over a pair of black slacks of her own. She easily and quickly slipped her arms into her dress coat to speed the process of getting Joshua to what he needed for his headache.

Still, the mayor had used even that small opportunity to launch into the reasons he was certain it would be in Joshua's interests to invest in Northbridge.

But once more Joshua cut him off.

"Absolutely," he agreed. "We'll discuss it all when I call you. But I really need to get to a dark room."

The mayor seemed satisfied as he opened the door

to bid them good night and let them out, keeping an eye on them as they returned to Cassie's car and got in.

It was only as Cassie backed down the mayor's driveway that the mayor finally went inside and closed the door.

When he had and they were no longer under scrutiny, Joshua stretched a long arm across the back of Cassie's seat and smiled at her in a way that showed no indication of pain or illness.

"Say thank you," he advised.

Cassie pulled away from the mayor's house and then took a closer look at Joshua. "You aren't sick."

"Never had a migraine in my life."

"You faked it?"

"You said I could be your date for your brother's rehearsal dinner if it wasn't for the mayor's party," Joshua reminded her.

"So you faked a migraine? With the *mayor,* of all people?"

"I'll make it up to him."

"And you were believable, too. I thought you had a headache."

He grinned as if it pleased him that he'd fooled her, too. "If I had had to spend the next few hours listening to that guy and his cohorts, I'm sure I would have developed one."

"So you lied to get out of there."

"I didn't lie altogether. I really will invest in some of their pet projects because I do like Northbridge, and it is in my best interest—and Alyssa's—for the mayor and everyone else to want to keep Alyssa's being here on the q.t. I just didn't see why we should have to sit there and listen to the whole presentation—especially when they weren't even waiting for cocktails to arrive before starting in. Usually people hitting me up for donations do it with more finesse. But since five minutes after we got there your mayor made it obvious what the purpose of that dinner was—which was exactly what I figured it was—and since I'll make sure he gets what he wants, this way, so do we."

"Because *we* want to go to Ben's rehearsal dinner?"

"Well, *I* do. I just figured you did, too."

"And if somebody at the rehearsal dinner lets word get out that you were there?"

Joshua leaned toward her to whisper in her ear as she drove in the direction of her family home. "You'd be surprised what I can get away with."

Like, for instance, sending little shivers down her spine with the feel of his breath against her ear and the scent of his light cologne wafting around her.

And he did get away with that because it wasn't as if she had moved away from him or told him to back off. The only thing she did was work to conceal the effect he had on her.

Then, on his own, he straightened up. "So, do I get to go to the rehearsal dinner?" he asked.

"I guess so."

"As your date?"

She gave him a sideways glance, recalling all that had gone into the game they'd played the night before about his being her date for Ben's dinner. About holding hands. And kissing good-night…

"Remember that I have four brothers," she said just in case Joshua actually did intend to hold her hand or show any kind of affection with her family around, knowing she'd only have that much more to answer for when he was gone. "And three of them will take you apart if they think you're getting out of line with me."

"And the fourth?"

"He'll put you back together again afterward, but it still won't be fun."

That made Joshua laugh. "The full meal deal," he joked, clearly not intimidated. "In other words, even if I *am* your date, I should keep my hands to myself or risk the wrath of the Walker brothers."

So he remembered their game, too.

"That's my advice."

"Okay. Hands off," he agreed, even taking his arm from her seat back.

But that still left Cassie wondering about the good-night kiss...

"You're missing your mother's house," Joshua pointed out when she drove past the place where she'd grown up.

There were a lot of cars parked on both sides of the street, but there was one spot directly in front that she could have used had she not been lost in thoughts of the end of the evening. And Joshua.

Trying not to let him know she'd been preoccupied that way, she said, "I'm a terrible parallel parker. I thought I'd turn around and park behind Ad, across the street."

Of course she also could have parked behind Ben's car in the driveway, but she didn't mention that and instead did as she'd said she would—making a U-turn at the corner and pulling up behind her older brother's SUV.

If Joshua noticed how odd her actions were, he didn't say anything. To continue to cover her tracks, Cassie began to talk about the rehearsal dinner itself.

"We were going to have it out in the backyard but the weather didn't cooperate—it's a risk this late in September. Now everyone will be inside. Luckily the weather report predicted a clearing and a big rise in temperatures for tomorrow and tomorrow night, though. The wedding and reception are supposed to be in the garden, too. There will be a tent and some space heaters set around here and there to keep away the evening chill, but if it's as cold as it is tonight, space heaters won't be enough and everything will have to be in the house again. Which would be kind of a mess because there are a lot more people coming to the wedding and the reception."

"Need a date for that?" Joshua said.

Cassie had babbled all the way through parking, stopping the engine, getting out of the car and heading for the house. But she stalled slightly as they climbed the porch steps to look at Joshua when he came out with that question.

"Are you offering?" she asked.

"Alyssa's new romance is hitting full steam and she'd be thrilled to have me off her hands for a real, live, Friday night date."

"So you just want something to keep yourself busy," Cassie surmised.

Joshua smiled too mischievously. "Believe me, anything that might get me busy with you, I'm in favor of."

Cassie fought a smile and tamped down the little thrill his words sent through her, playing it cool. "Maybe we'd better see how you do tonight," she answered as if the thought of having Joshua take her to Ben's wedding didn't sound like the best idea ever.

The wedding rehearsal was over, but the buffet dinner was just beginning as they entered the Walker family home. The wedding party and their spouses or dates and kids, the extended family of the bride, and several close friends were milling around with plates in hand, finding spots to sit and eat, or heading for the kitchen to get to the food.

Everyone was surprised to see them; Cassie made sure word spread that Joshua had played sick to get them out of the mayor's dinner and that that fact should be kept confidential. A good laugh was had by all over that and Joshua seemed to come out of it a hero for having gotten Cassie home for this occasion. It also gained him points with the Walker brothers, who began to treat him like they did one another, making it apparent that they were accepting him and giving him their stamp of approval.

A stamp of approval that Cassie would have been glad for Joshua to have under different circumstances.

But these *weren't* different circumstances, she reminded herself.

Here today, gone tomorrow—or at least in a few days. That was Joshua.

And she needed to remember that.

Chapter Eleven

The rehearsal dinner and party lasted until about ten that night before the dishes were cleared and guests began to leave.

Cassie made sure her mother's kitchen and dining room were completely clean and ready for the caterers, who would arrive the next day to do the wedding food, before she asked Joshua if he was ready to go, too.

He was, so they said their good-nights—but not without Joshua leaving with a whole lot of encouragement to attend the wedding the next evening.

"That's up to Cassie," he said at the door with her mother, Ben, Ad and Reid all standing there to see them out. "She said she'd have to see how I did tonight before she'd let me come tomorrow."

Putting her on the spot like that was exactly what one of her brothers would have done. Only had Joshua been one of her brothers, she would have punched him. As it was, she narrowed her eyes at him and said, "Just saying that may have cost you, smart guy."

Joshua grinned as her mother and brothers sided with him, telling him he was welcome whether Cassie said so or not.

"Come on, you pain in the neck," she joked then. "I'm taking you home before you get me into any more trouble."

Joshua thanked her mother for everything, said goodnight and only then did they leave.

"*Will* you take me home?" he said as they returned to her car.

"Where else would I take you? Out into the country to leave you stranded on a deserted road the way you deserve after that last gambit?"

"I meant, will you take me to *your* home? I have something stashed in your bushes I want to give you and then I'll walk to the chancellor's cottage."

The man was full of surprises. "You have something stashed in my bushes?"

He only smiled as he held open the driver's side door for her and waited for her to get behind the wheel.

He refused to tell her what he had stashed in her bushes—or even if there really was anything hidden there—despite attempts by Cassie the entire way back to her house to get the information out of him.

But once she'd parked in her own driveway again, Joshua wasted no time getting out of the car and indeed going to one of the clumps of bushes that bracketed both sides of her front stoop. He pulled out a bottle of wine just as Cassie joined him.

"I wanted to say thanks for everything you've done this week, and to give you a little housewarming present," he said, holding out the ribbon-wrapped bottle to her.

Cassie knew nothing about wine but since the date on the label wasn't recent, she guessed it was better than the premixed sangria she generally bought on sale at the local liquor store.

"You didn't have to do that," she said as she accepted the gift.

"I told you I wanted to."

"Thank you. That's really thoughtful."

Cassie pretended to study the label when, in fact, much more complicated things were going through her mind.

Then she glanced from the bottle to Joshua. "It always seems a shame if it doesn't get opened and shared with the person who brought it," she said, giving in to the opportunity to extend the evening that felt as if it had only just begun now that they weren't with a whole slew of other people.

"It is my own personal favorite," Joshua commented.

That morsel of encouragement was all it took to push her over the edge of her decision. "Would you like to come in and break it open?"

He smiled as if he'd been waiting to hear those words. "I would."

"The place is a mess," she warned. "I haven't had time to unpack anything this week and—"

"I don't mind. All we need is a corkscrew and a couple of glasses. We can even sit on the floor if we need to."

"I do have a couch. But the glasses will have to be paper and I'll have to dig through boxes for a corkscrew."

"I'm okay with paper cups," he said, giving Cassie the impression that nothing she might say at that point was going to dissuade him.

Not that she wanted to. And because she didn't want to, she unlocked her door and stepped inside.

"Come in, but you'd better stay put until I get to a lamp or you might fall over something."

She'd been navigating the boxes and unplaced furniture all week, so she knew the route and it took her only a moment to reach a pole lamp in the corner and turn it on. Once she had, she discovered Joshua removing his coat and tossing it over the top of three boxes stacked on each other as he glanced around.

"I know it must not compare to anything you live in or frequent, but—"

"I like it," he said, cutting her off before she could say anything else about her modest new house.

"I like it, too. It's small but cute and functional and practical and perfect for me," she finished, wondering herself if there was more of a message in that than she'd consciously intended. For them both, maybe.

She removed her own coat and tossed it on the rolltop desk near the lamp. "Why don't you sit down while I get the corkscrew and glasses?" she invited. "Just go around those boxes you're looking over, make a left and then a quick right and you can get to the sofa."

He did as she'd instructed while she went to the

kitchen at the rear of the house, returning after a surprisingly speedy search with a corkscrew and two small plastic-coated paper cups with butterflies on them.

Joshua was standing in front of the couch waiting for her. Cassie handed the wine bottle back to him and said, "I'll let you do the honors. I usually wreck the cork."

He accomplished removing the cork intact in no time and set the bottle on the cardboard box positioned in front of the couch like a coffee table.

"Let's let it breathe a few minutes," he suggested, waiting for Cassie to sit before he did.

And then there they were, both of them in the center of the plaid sofa, angled slightly towards each other, Joshua's left arm stretched along the top of the cushions, and Cassie suddenly felt awkward and wondered what to say.

Until her gaze fell to the butterfly cups she'd set on the makeshift coffee table, too, and then it suddenly struck her that they were sitting in a fort of cardboard packing boxes, their enclave only dimly lit by a bare-bulb lamp awaiting the discovery of its shade, about to drink probably expensive wine from paper cups. Which was when past experience gave her something to say after all.

"I'm sorry about this. I didn't realize just how much of a mess I've been living in or just how bad it all looks until now."

"I've moved before," he said. "I kind of like this stage—roughing it—at first. It's fun. And it makes you appreciate it all the more when everything gets cleared and cleaned and situated."

"True," Cassie agreed, wondering if that was actually how he felt or if he was just being polite.

He poured the wine then and handed her a paper cup, settling back the way he'd been before with his own glass.

Cassie tried the wine and gave it her stamp of approval. "Fruity, not too dry, I like it."

"Good," Joshua said as if it genuinely pleased him that she did.

Then he took the lead. "I learned some very interesting things tonight," he said, clearly as a segue intended to intrigue her.

"Let's see, you spent a lot of time with my brothers—" more than he'd spent with her, to her dismay "—so you could have learned how to burp the alphabet from Ad—his talent at twelve. Or how to shoot pop bottle rockets under cars—one of Ben's early infractions. Or—"

"What I learned had to do with you. And Brandon Adams."

He knew Brandon's last name. Cassie was certain she hadn't told him what it was. So her brothers really had talked considerably tonight. That was much worse than burping the alphabet.

"I'm sorry. That's the last thing they should have told you about. Sometimes my family—"

"I like your family," he was quick to come to their defense. "To tell you the truth, it *wasn't* your family who brought him up. A couple of other people made comments about your used-to-be fiancé—" Joshua leaned forward to confide, "That's right, I found out that's who the infamous *Brandon* was." He sat back, but not terribly far back. "So I asked your brothers about him when I got the chance."

Cassie sighed and opted for discovering just how well-informed Joshua was about her past. "What did they tell you?" she asked.

"That two years ago Brandon Adams—big deal investment broker—was persuaded by the college to come to Northbridge to do a series of seminars. That you took his seminars. That sparks flew even though he was eight years older than you were. That a whirlwind romance ensued—flowers, long phone conversations, trips for you to see him, for him to see you. That you liked the same books, music, movies, the whole bit—"

"Somebody did way, way too much talking tonight."

"And they told me that you thought the two of you were perfect for each other," Joshua continued. "That you got engaged. That he conceded to having the wedding in Northbridge, even though by then everyone knew he was looking down on them and the town. But since he seemed to genuinely care for you and he treated you well, your family agreed within the ranks to ignore his arrogance. I learned that something happened at the rehearsal dinner the night before the wedding and everything was called off. I just didn't find out *what* happened. Or how the pigs in a blanket fit in. My informants kept getting interrupted and then you dragged me away before we could get to that part."

"I knew you were holed up with my brothers a lot tonight but I had no idea it was long enough to get all that out of them," Cassie said.

"What can I say? I'm good and the beer was flowing

pretty freely." Joshua refilled both paper cups with the wine they were sharing in lieu of beer. "So. Any of it not true?" he asked then.

"No. That's the story in a nutshell. Brandon came to Northbridge, we hit it off, bing bam boom, the next thing I knew he was asking me to marry him and I was saying yes."

"And then…" Joshua said. "Aren't you going to fill me in on what happened at the rehearsal dinner and why pigs in a blanket are such a big deal?"

Cassie sipped her wine for courage, wishing her brothers would have kept their mouths shut. The only reason any information about Brandon should have reached Joshua was if it had come through her.

But it was too late now and seeing as how he already knew everything but the ending, she decided she might as well provide him with that.

"What happened at the rehearsal dinner *was* the pigs in a blanket," she said. "And my brothers were right, Brandon *did* look down on them and Northbridge and everyone in it. He was from an old money family back east—"

"I know. I know him."

That surprised her enough for her to stare at Joshua. And note just how handsome he was—something she could hardly believe she was aware of even in the midst of reliving the most painful ending of any relationship she'd ever had and the shock of hearing that Joshua Cantrell actually knew her former fiancé.

"You know him?" she said.

"It really is a small world. The New York branch of

his family's brokerage house handles a lot of my investments. Brandon doesn't do it personally, but I've had dinner with him and with his father on occasion when they were wooing my business."

"Then it's probably more obvious to you than it was to me that he and I were as ill-suited for each other as any two people could be."

Joshua made a face. "Why would that be obvious to me?"

This time Cassie thought there was no doubt he was only being polite.

"Oh, please. It's as plain as the nose on your face," she said. "Brandon and his family are your kind, not mine."

"My *kind?* What kind is that?"

"You—and they—are high society and I'm... Well, I was told I'm nothing but a country bumpkin who hides it well."

"Who said that?" Joshua demanded as if he were ready to defend her, too.

"Brandon. That night of the rehearsal dinner. Up until then he would affectionately refer to me as his *country girl.* But then it got amended."

Joshua's brows came together over the bridge of his perfect nose. "He didn't honestly call you a country bumpkin."

"He did. In the heat of anger, but he did."

"You're not a bumpkin."

"I'm also not old money or high society or a jet-setter or any of the things people like you and Brandon are."

"Now it's me and Brandon—joined at the hip just because I know him?"

"Not joined at the hip, but still, big-city wheelers and dealers."

"Come on," Joshua said as if she couldn't possibly be serious. "I admit that our paths have crossed but Brandon Adams is…" Joshua hesitated then seemed to give in. "I'm sorry to say it about somebody you cared for even once upon a time, but Brandon Adams has always struck me as pompous and pretentious. I'm surprised you saw anything in him and I'm figuring that because he fell for you he showed you a side of himself that I've never seen from him. But you're putting the two of us in the same category?"

"You operate in the same circles, don't you?"

"Yes, but—"

"Probably go to the same restaurants, have homes in the same zip codes around the world, have the same tax bracket, maybe even date some of the same women…"

Joshua rolled his eyes. "We're nothing alike."

Their personalities might be different—Joshua did seem to have been accepted by her brothers and that was not something Brandon had aspired to or made any attempts to accomplish. But as far as Cassie was concerned, there were enough similarities between Joshua and Brandon to make Joshua as unquestionably off-limits and wrong for her as Brandon had ended up being. Which was really what she was thinking.

She just didn't see the point in arguing it.

So she didn't.

"Okay, you're nothing alike," she conceded to appease him.

He looked somewhat skeptical but let it rest. "Back

to the rehearsal dinner and the pigs in a blanket," he reminded.

Cassie finished her second cup of wine and Joshua again filled it.

Needing another confidence booster, she took a sip, then returned to the subject.

"I wanted to get married in Northbridge with my friends and family," she explained. "Brandon wasn't thrilled with it, but he said if I'd let his family give us a second reception at their New Hampshire home, his parents, brother and sister would come here for the actual ceremony. That was the plan—a small, cozy, informal wedding and reception here with my side, a bigger, splashier reception there with the rest of his extended family and friends. And since no one but his parents, brother and sister were coming for the Northbridge events, we didn't think they should have to put on the re-hearsal dinner the way they might have under other cir-cumstances. So my mom offered to do that, too."

"Like tonight."

"Except that it was in July and so we decided to just have a barbecue. Which apparently meant something different to Brandon than it did to me."

"To you it meant pigs in a blanket?" Joshua guessed.

Cassie was beginning to feel light-headed so she set her half-empty paper cup on the cardboard box coffee table in order not to be tempted to drink any more.

"The barbecue was casual," she said, ignoring the pigs in a blanket question for a moment. "To us, that meant chips and dips. Carrot and celery sticks. Ribs and corn on the cob cooked on the grill. Potato salad. Baked beans—

casual. And Mom made pigs in a blanket appetizers to put out with the chips and dips and veggie sticks."

Cassie couldn't help the forlorn tone that came into her voice because even now it seemed unbelievable that her feelings for Brandon, the feelings she'd believed he had for her, had gone by the wayside because of anything as ridiculous as tiny hot dogs wrapped in dough.

"The menu sounds good to me," Joshua said to prompt her to continue when her own emotions stalled her. "But Brandon thought it was *too* casual?"

"He couldn't believe that anyone would serve anything called pigs in a blanket to anyone, let alone to guests. Let alone to guests at a wedding rehearsal dinner, no matter how casual. And—especially—let alone to his family. He was appalled and outraged."

To say the least.

"Did he make a scene?" Joshua asked.

"No, he wouldn't do that. First, he just kept apologizing and apologizing to his parents and brother and sister—quietly, so my family wouldn't hear, but I was right there, so I heard it. He kept saying that if he'd had any idea that that was what *casual* meant here, even when it came to a *wedding,* he would have made sure it wasn't allowed. He was just so completely ashamed of me, of *my* family…."

Cassie's voice caught and she cleared her throat.

"What about his folks and brother and sister? How did they react?"

"About as badly. His mother and sister just kept exchanging glances as if they couldn't believe what they were in the middle of. His brother made a lot of sarcastic and very cutting remarks. I overheard his father tell Brandon that it was just lucky that no one else had come for this, that *their* people wouldn't ever have to know that was how the wedding was."

Joshua flinched. "How had they treated you up to then? Had they not approved or been standoffish or—"

"I'd met them only once, before they got to North-bridge. Brandon had taken me to New Hampshire for a long weekend. But they were nice to me while I was there. I was a little in awe of their house and the way they lived, but they seemed okay with the fact that I came from a working-class background. I even said a few things along the lines of how different they'd find the way we live in Northbridge and his mother said she was sure it was all very quaint. Apparently that wasn't how she saw it once she got here."

"So they honestly canceled a wedding because you served them pigs in a blanket?" Joshua asked, still clearly having trouble grasping that.

"We made it through the dinner. But afterward Brandon and I had a huge fight—that was when the country bumpkin thing was said. And that was when I really knew that it wasn't going to work out between us. I was the first to suggest calling off the wedding, but even if I hadn't done it, Brandon would have. I could see in his face that he couldn't go through with marrying me. It was as if he were seeing me for the first time and didn't like what he saw. We agreed to call it off."

"And ever since then your poor mom has felt responsible because she served pigs in a blanket?" Joshua said with a sympathetic expression that went far in making Cassie feel better.

"Yes. For a while she went around saying that she'd ruined my life with them," Cassie said with a laugh. "And even though I've told her a million times that that isn't true, that everything would not have turned out just fine had there never been pigs in a blanket, that something else would have eventually triggered Brandon into realizing how different we were. It still comes up now and then."

"Like when she discovered you'd brought me for a lunch of pigs in a blanket—"

Cassie had to laugh again at the irony of that. "She hasn't made them since that night and here it was, the first time she thought it was safe to do it again, and I brought home another man. She was sure she was wrecking things for me all over again."

Joshua flinched. "My cover story is to blame for that, isn't it?"

"Yes, but you made up for it by knowing what pigs in a blanket are and by eating as many of them as my brothers did. Brandon didn't have a clue what they were until I told him and neither he nor any of his family would touch them. That's probably why my brothers were willing to tell you the Brandon stuff—the pigs in a blanket bought your way into the inner circle," Cassie said as if that were a coveted place to be.

"I'm honored," Joshua joked.

"So there you have it," she concluded then. "The complete history of my fateful rehearsal dinner and the pigs in a blanket issue."

"And I probably tarnished your enjoyment of your brother's party tonight by bringing it up."

"It's okay," she said. And somehow it was. Just as so many things seemed to take a backseat when she was with Joshua. Even her failed engagement didn't have quite the impact it had once had now that she was sitting only inches away from him.

"Your brothers are worried I'm the rebound guy," he said then, one arched eyebrow adding his own curiosity to the mix.

"It's been over with Brandon for more than a year. I've seen a couple of guys—one of them for five months. I'm past the rebound stage."

"But you were too afraid to bring either of the rebound guys home? Because I heard that I'm the first since Brandon."

And he sounded proud of that.

"I wasn't afraid at all. Both of the guys I've been with are Northbridge natives who know my family. They didn't need to be taken home to meet anyone. Besides, I wasn't that serious about them."

Joshua grinned. "But me? Me, you took home."

"Not the same," she reminded him. "We aren't *dating*."

"I beg your pardon," he pretended to be insulted. "Your *date* was exactly what I was tonight. Or have you forgotten?"

Cassie couldn't help smiling at his show of offense. "You know what I mean."

"That you're a fraud. First you say I can come as your date tonight and hold your hand and touch you and really *be* your date. Then you warn me that your brothers will beat the snot out of me if I even stand too close to you. Now you're saying I'm not even technically your date. You're a fickle woman. A fraud and a fickle woman."

"Guilty as charged," Cassie confessed, playing along.

"So I guess I'd better get out of here before you do any more damage to my self-esteem."

Oh. She hadn't expected that just yet. When it still seemed so early. Even if it wasn't. It also still seemed as if she hadn't had enough time with him. And she wasn't any more eager to have him go now than she had been when they'd returned from Ben's rehearsal dinner.

But Joshua really was ready to leave because he stood. And since she couldn't very well tell him she wanted him to stay—and *shouldn't* be feeling or thinking that anyway—she stood, too, following behind as he circumvented the maze of boxes to get to the door and retrieve his coat.

Something was different tonight, though, Cassie thought then. It was different in that Joshua had kept a certain amount of distance throughout the party, spending more time with her brothers than with her. And it was different now, too, than the end of the last few evenings.

Not that she wasn't still sensing the same kind of electrical charge passing between them, because she was. And there had been the same level of flirting, of teasing, of innuendo. But it was as if Joshua had himself more under control. As if he was working harder at resisting that draw that was usually pulling them together by now.

Which was for the best, Cassie told herself. Especially when she'd proven so weak herself every other night.

Yet she was aware of the letdown that settled over her as he shrugged those big, broad shoulders into his impeccable cashmere coat.

"Tomorrow is jam-packed with Parents' Week stuff," Joshua was saying as he did. "Alyssa and I are doing it all together and since I'm sure you have a lot of pre-wedding things to do, don't worry about me. Alyssa firmly committed to dinner together tomorrow night, too—which counts me out for Ben's wedding ceremony. But if you aren't opposed, I'd like to come to the reception afterward. I'd like to see you. If that's okay."

So something was different, but not completely different if he was again trying to prearrange more time with her.

And because he wasn't couching it tonight in any kind of game, Cassie couldn't hide her own desire to be with him, either.

So she didn't. Despite the concern that she shouldn't be admitting what she was about to…

"I'd like that," she said. "You can bring Alyssa, too, if—"

"I'm sure she'll want to rush to the new boyfriend as soon as she can."

Cassie smiled and tried for some of that levity and game-playing that had served her before. "Ah, you're just looking to keep yourself busy again when your sister ditches you, huh?"

Joshua smiled, as well, but there was no joking around in his expression as he looked down into her eyes. "Believe me, I'd be in a whole lot less trouble if I just went to a movie or stayed in with a good book to keep me busy. But no, as much as I know what I *should* do, I just can't make myself go without being with you at all tomorrow. Promises or no promises."

He said that last part more to himself than to her but Cassie needed to explore it anyway. "What kind of promises did you make and to whom?"

"Alyssa. I promised her that I wouldn't do this with you."

Cassie recalled the conversation they'd had earlier in the week about his sister's concerns for her. "Is this Alyssa worrying about me needing protection from you again?"

"Not protection from me, protection from the circus that usually surrounds me. But so far we've dodged that bullet and…" He shook his head, his crystalline silver eyes never leaving hers. "Well, I do have an invitation to the wedding, after all," he finished, retreating to a bit of subterfuge himself.

He raised a hand to cup the side of her face and shook his head. "I just have too good a time with you," he added in a quieter voice, as if he were confiding in her.

Or had his voice become quieter—sexier—for some other reason?

"Brandon Adams was crazy to let you go," he said then.

Just before he leaned down to kiss her.

Cassie didn't know what Joshua had promised his sister or if that was why things had been different tonight, but there was nothing held back from that kiss. His lips were parted right from the start. The hand at her cheek combed through her hair to cradle the back of her head, and his other arm went around her to pull her near enough for her breasts to brush his chest.

Not that Cassie held anything in reserve, either, in

spite of the little voice coming from the recesses of her mind, telling her to think better of this. All it took was Joshua's mouth on hers to make her own lips part. All it took was the feel of his powerful arms around her, of his awe-inspiring body so close to hers, to make her own hands plunge inside his coat and find their way to his back.

All it took was his tongue to come in search of hers, for hers to meet him, match him, and play the cat-and-mouse game he initiated.

All it took was a few moments of that kiss that began where the kiss of the previous night had left off for it to deepen, to intensify, to turn into more than a simple good-night kiss.

And when it did, mouths opened wide and bodies pressed so near that Cassie's breasts were flattened to his hard, honed chest. Her nipples tightened and introduced themselves, and her blood seemed to run hot and fast through her veins, awakening something inside her that seemed to have been sleeping. Something that shot desire through her and rendered her putty in its hands.

Putty in Joshua's hands, Cassie thought, if only he would take them from their safe moorings and let them roam. Let them roam to her rear end. To her breasts. To clothes that she suddenly wished would vanish. To skin that was dying to feel his bare flesh against it.

With that in mind, Cassie slid her hands to his front and then let them climb to his shoulders, to his biceps, easing his coat off and allowing it to carelessly fall to the floor.

Joshua must have taken that as the sign it was half intended to be, because at least one of his hands did some traveling then. From her hair to the side of her neck. To her shoulder, where he spent a titillating moment massaging, kneading and giving her what she hoped was a sneak preview. To her upper arm where he did the same thing, only more firmly, before he slipped that hand to the spot Cassie was wishing he would, to her breast.

But no matter how good it was to finally have his hand there, it would have been better without the lace top and built-in bra still between them.

Which Joshua must have thought, too, because he didn't wait for any more signs from Cassie. He let his hand drop to the hem of her shirt and effortlessly slipped underneath it and upward again....

Cassie had to fight to keep herself from moaning when that smooth, adept hand came into first contact with her bare breast. But, oh, what a fight it took! It just felt so amazing to have his warm skin on hers. To have his fingers working her flesh, teasing her nipple, gently turning it and twisting it and persuading it to knot into an even tauter cluster of nerve endings that were alert all at once and responding to the wonders of his touch.

A touch that felt better than she could believe. A touch that was the perfect blend of tenderness and toughness. Of pressure and featherlight strokes. A touch that somehow managed to raise her desire to new heights with each grasp, each motion, each perfectly applied compression and caress.

A touch she wanted to feel everywhere. Over every inch of her body.

But not standing there at her front door, amidst towers of cardboard boxes.

She wanted to be lying down. Beside Joshua. With arms and legs entwined. With naked body against naked body. With hands and mouths and tongues all free to play…

But it was the thought of her sheets that stopped her.

Not that they weren't clean, because they were. They were clean, pale blue sheets.

Plain, clean, pale blue sheets that suited Cassie just fine. But she had had no idea what their thread count was when Brandon had been introduced to them and complained that they weren't good enough.

And if they hadn't been good enough for Brandon, they weren't good enough for Joshua.

And Joshua, like Brandon, could well think that she wasn't good enough, either….

That was the real reminder that that little voice in the recesses of her mind had been trying to get through and it finally made it.

Loud and clear.

Joshua would hate her sheets as much as Brandon had. And eventually he could hate her, too. Just as Brandon had…

"Oh, no, wait. This can't happen," she said after interrupting their kiss and dropping her chin to avert her face, her lips, from this man she wanted but knew she couldn't have. "You made promises to your sister. I made promises to myself…."

"What promises did you make to yourself?" he asked in a deep, deep voice.

"Not to do this," she answered simply and without giving any details because she didn't want him to have anything to refute.

And he didn't. He merely lowered his brow to the top of her head and slipped his hand out from under her lacey top, placing it lightly to her back with his other one.

"You're probably right," he agreed, sounding as if he'd reluctantly come to that conclusion.

But Cassie knew that if she stayed where she was, still in his arms, feeling the heat of his breath in her hair for much longer, she was going to convince them both that she was wrong and do something she shouldn't do.

So she slipped out of his arms and bent over to take his coat off the floor and hold it for him to get into again.

He didn't do that, either, though. Instead he took it from her hands. "I think I need to do some cooling off."

Cassie nodded and finally hazarded a glance up at him, wishing like mad that just one look at the man didn't make her heart actually beat faster. But it did. Again. Especially when he smiled a small smile that bathed her in liquid gold.

"Like I said," he nearly whispered, "I just have too good a time with you."

"Yeah, it's a problem," she agreed.

He leaned forward and kissed her again, chastely this time, there and gone before it could evolve into anything more, and then he opened her door.

"I'll see you tomorrow night," he said.

It was on the tip of Cassie's tongue to ask if it was wise for him to come to Ben's reception after all. After what had just happened. After what else might have happened.

But she didn't do it.

She couldn't.

Not when it might cause him not to show up.

Not when she still wanted him as badly as she did.

Whether she could have him or not.

Instead, she merely nodded and watched him leave.

And told herself that no matter how tempting it was, she was absolutely not going to go out tomorrow and buy new sheets.

But it was very, very—*very*—tempting…

Chapter Twelve

The wedding of Cassie's twin brother Ben and her old friend Clair Cabot was short and sweet. The weather co-operated to provide a beautiful evening for the seven o'clock ceremony in the backyard of the Walker family home. Wildflowers were woven around the poles that held the white tent overhead and decorated the lattice arch backdrop for the ceremony.

The groom and all his brothers—who were being called his Pack of Best Men so no one had their feelings hurt by being reduced to mere groomsmen—wore tuxedos. Clair's dress was a simple, elegant, sleeveless satin A-line, floor-length gown with twenty-four pearl buttons down the back.

Cassie was the maid of honor and, along with the

other two bridesmaids, wore a mauve-colored sleeveless dress embossed with a floral design. It had a wide V-neckline that required a strapless bra underneath, and ended at the point with a scarf tie that led the eye down to the drop waist. The skirt was two layers—a lining that fell to Cassie's knees, and a sheer overskirt that ended just below that in a handkerchief hem.

Her shoes were a pair of four-inch high-heeled mules with mesh uppers topped off by kid leather roses.

It was definitely an outfit she would wear again because it fit her to a *T* and made her feel uncommonly sexy.

Her lipstick matched her dress, she'd used a touch more blush than usual, darker mascara and some eyeliner to define her turquoise eyes. She was even pleased that her hair had turned out exactly the way she liked it best—curled under at the ends but with just enough poof and body to make it bounce, with the bangs swept to brush just the edge of her left eyebrow.

"I now present to you all, Mr. and Mrs. Walker," the minister announced after the vows and rings had been exchanged, as well as the kiss.

Everyone clapped and someone whistled, and as Ben and Clair made the return trip down the aisle formed by white wooden folding chairs, their guests blew varying sizes of rainbow-hued bubbles at them.

The receiving line formed at the rear of the tent while the chairs were moved to make way for the band, the dance floor and the tables that guests went to sit around once they'd offered their congratulations to the new couple.

By then, Cassie was keeping a close watch on the gate to the south of the house.

She'd given herself permission not to fret about how glad she was that Joshua was coming tonight. Parents' Week was drawing to a close and she knew that he would be leaving Northbridge any day now. Maybe even to-morrow. So her time with him was rapidly waning and after spending this past week trying to keep her attraction to him in check, she knew that the temptation he presented was about to end. He would go wherever in the world he was headed next, she would resume her normal routine and get her house set up, and life would go on. Unchanged.

Given that, she'd decided she might as well just sit back and enjoy whatever few hours she had left with him.

Besides, it *was* Ben's and Clair's wedding—an evening when it was nice that she would have an escort and someone to share it with.

If only he would get there!

The buffet table was laden with food but not until the bride and groom headed in that direction did the rest of the guests follow suit. Since Cassie knew Joshua would have eaten with his sister before he arrived, she made her way there, too, paying more attention to that gate than to what she was filling her plate with.

She'd just reached the end of the buffet table where the wedding cake was displayed when she spotted Joshua. The elation that flooded her probably should have served as a warning, but it didn't. She was just so happy to see him. So happy that she merely smiled when other female guests' jaws actually dropped at that initial glimpse of him joining them under the tent.

He looked that good.

Tall and straight, he walked in with the bearing of a

male runway model dressed in a dark, dark charcoal-gray suit so impeccably tailored it put the tuxedos to shame. The jacket was worn over a flawless white shirt and white tie, and fitted his shoulders to perfection, hugging his torso just enough to define his narrow waist before finishing above a pair of slacks that accentuated his long legs.

He was freshly shaven; his black hair looked as if it had been trimmed for the occasion. And seeing him was all it took for Cassie to lose total awareness of everything and everyone but Joshua, whose eyes were on her and her alone as he made a path to her.

He stopped in front of her at the end of the buffet table and let his silver gaze take in her shoes, her dress, her hair and face, giving his approval with a smile even before he said, "You and that dress are going to make my heart stop."

She couldn't let him know the sight of him and that compliment were likely to have the same effect on her so she only said, "You better be careful then, because there are two more of me around here."

Joshua located both of the other bridesmaids and then resumed staring at Cassie.

"Nope, you're the only one putting me at risk."

Her ear-to-ear grin probably gave her away, but Cassie couldn't suppress it.

She did, however, change courses by holding up her plate of food and saying, "Are you hungry?"

"I just finished eating with Alyssa. At your brother Ad's restaurant. But I saw the champagne fountain when I came in. Why don't you find us a place to sit and I'll get two glasses?"

Cassie spotted a small table in a far corner of the tent that was free and nodded towards it. "I'll be there."

She had barely tasted her poached salmon before Joshua, carrying two plastic champagne glasses, met her at the table they had to themselves.

"This is nice," Joshua commented as he sat across from her.

Cassie's gaze dropped to the plastic glasses that Brandon would have loathed and then she looked back at Joshua. "You don't mean that. I know this can't compare to what you're used to."

"I've been to some big deal weddings," he confirmed. "But none of them were mine and if they had been, I'd have opted for something like this—family and close friends, your mom's garden all around us, fun, relaxed. I think this is great."

Cassie wasn't sure she believed him. But rather than press the point, she decided he'd given her an opening to ask about something else. Something she was dying to know.

So she said, "How come none of the weddings *were* yours? I thought I read or heard something a while ago about your being engaged."

His expression changed with that question but she couldn't read it. And he didn't immediately give her an answer. He drank some champagne.

Cassie was reasonably sure she'd hit a nerve.

Then, as she picked at her food, he said, "I *was* engaged. A while ago."

And that was it. No details.

Reminding herself that he had no obligation to tell

her anything, Cassie said, "I understand. It's none of my business."

"No, it isn't that. I'm sorry if I made you feel that way. It just isn't something easy for me to talk about."

"Oh. A bad breakup of your own, huh?"

"Not bad in the sense you're thinking—fighting or cheating or name-calling. So much worse than that."

He was only whetting her appetite. But she was hesitant to pry now.

She was thrilled, though, when Joshua continued without it.

"I *was* engaged. To a woman named Jennie Burg."

"The name doesn't ring a bell but I probably saw her picture if it was on the cover of a checkout-stand paper." Although Cassie had no actual memory of a face.

"She wasn't a celebrity or anything. She was someone I met through work—the manager of one of my shoe plants. But we hit it off. We enjoyed each other's company. Liked each other…"

There was affection in Joshua's tone that told her the relationship hadn't ended because he'd tired of the woman. Which made Cassie feel a jealousy she knew she wasn't entitled to. It was tempered only by the fact that along with the affection in his voice, there was also the echo of regret.

"We dated. Got serious. It happened pretty fast—I guess most of the big turning points in my life have. But it was also about the same time the press started hounding me. Before I really had any kind of grasp of what that was all about or where it could lead. I also didn't realize that when the photographers and rag reporters get hold of you, they like to spin you in whatever direction makes them the most money. And that if they decide a negative spin sells more magazines or newspapers, that's what they'll do. No matter what it takes or who it hurts."

Cassie wasn't very hungry so she pushed her plate away and merely sipped her champagne. "Like I've said before, I haven't really kept up on every detail about you, but my impression has been that the press is in love with you."

"Mmm. With me. As a single man about town with someone new—and newsworthy—for every issue."

"But getting engaged went against that?"

"Not so much at first. It gave them a new angle— Most Eligible Bachelor Off The Market—that sort of thing. And if Jennie had been a model or an actress or some big sports darling, it would have been different. But Jennie was just Jennie. She was from a middle-class background. She was pretty—beautiful to me— but she didn't photograph well. She didn't have a stripper's body made possible through plastic surgery. She didn't have any flash. Any outward pizzazz. And every time one of the picture hogs photographed her, she was usually trying to duck out of the way, or she was flinching or squinting or doing something to get out of the spotlight. That made her seem unattractive, which was what kicked off the negative. My little ugly duckling—that's what they started calling her."

"Ouch."

"It was hurtful to her," he acknowledged.

"So she wasn't who the media wanted for you," Cassie summarized.

"Right. And as a result, they started looking for ways to put that negative spin on her. Some of it purely lies, and some of it not…"

Cassie gave him a moment because he seemed to need it. She went for two more glasses of champagne.

When she returned she said, "Did they dig up dirt on her or what?"

"Not on her. Initially, at any rate. On her mother. Her mother had had some problems with alcohol. She'd had an accident while under the influence, a man was hurt. She was arrested. She'd lost her driver's license, been court-ordered into rehab—"

"Sounds like prime celebrity stuff," Cassie observed.

"Sure, but it's bad enough when some movie star has their mug shot on the front of a national publication. They're in the public eye, they've chosen that. For Jennie—and her family—to have her mother's mug shot there was worse. Plus, the headlines hinted at horrible things—things like maybe her mother had hit and killed a child while driving drunk, things about my buying her way out of jail, things that had never happened. And even the portions that had any amount of truth to them were slanted to make everything look even worse than it had been."

"And I'm sure it must have been bad enough for her family to have gone through anyway."

"Exactly."

"How awful," Cassie said.

"Once the tabloids got started, they wouldn't let up,"

Joshua continued. "Then they began to say that Jennie was an alcoholic like her mother, to hound her even worse. They fabricated pictures that were supposed to show her falling down drunk in a gutter, or drinking straight out of a wine bottle half-wrapped in a paper bag like a derelict. They reported that she'd been arrested for drunk and disorderly conduct. That she'd abused hotel personnel and destroyed public property on wild benders. It was ridiculous."

"And more than Jennie could take?" Cassie guessed.

"She was literally under a very public attack. She'd also gone through some depression during the worst of her mother's problems and had begun to take antidepressants, to see a therapist. That got out, too, but blown out of proportion, and…" He frowned down at his glass and shook his head. "It all took its toll."

"She couldn't go through with marrying you," Cassie said, thinking she was finishing for him.

But Joshua shook his head again, his expression even more dire. "Like I said, Jennie had had some emotional lows even before this. Her mother was sober and out of trouble before Jennie and I met, but Jennie still felt in need of the medication and the counseling. Which was okay," he was quick to add. "She's just a person who takes things very seriously. Who internalizes more than she should. Who could get the blues worse than most of us. But to me, the antidepressants and the therapy meant she was working on it. Working on herself. Taking responsibility for what was going on with her, and I respected that."

"But then she came under public attack," Cassie repeated Joshua's words.

"And she bottomed out," he said. "The depression became an even bigger problem and the medication wasn't helping. She switched to different drugs, increased her therapy sessions, and I did everything I could. But it wasn't enough. Especially in the face of the continuing harassment and the exposure by the press that she was seeing a shrink. She ended up trying to commit suicide. She slit her wrists. In the bathtub of the apartment we shared at the time." Another shake of the head and an even harsher frown. "And Alyssa found her."

"Oh," Cassie nearly whispered as the impact struck her.

"It was bad all the way around," Joshua said, his tone sounding as tortured as he must have felt at the time.

"Is that what you were talking about when you made that reference earlier this week about something happening that rocked you and Alyssa both?" Cassie asked.

"Yeah. It was…" Yet another shake of the head, as if he still couldn't believe what had gone on. "It was about as bad as losing our parents, even though Jennie didn't die. She was institutionalized. Alyssa was a basket case herself—she and Jennie had gotten close by then and finding her that way hit the poor kid hard. She needed counseling, too, for a few months afterward. The whole thing was just…horrible."

"And what didn't survive was your relationship with Jennie," Cassie said.

"There was no way the relationship *could* survive. Jennie was terrified of what being connected to me caused. Alyssa was traumatized by finding Jennie and—

at only sixteen then—was uncomfortable about the thought of having Jennie in our lives after that. The whole thing was a huge mess."

"And how did you feel?"

Joshua shrugged. "I'd been the reason it had all happened. I still cared for Jennie but more than love, I felt guilty and helpless and responsible for the lousy experience both she and Alyssa had gone through. Those feelings didn't seem like a firm foundation for the future. Plus, it was more than clear that I couldn't inflict what came with my life on Jennie anymore. She wasn't strong enough to deal with it, to withstand it unscathed. She and I agreed to go our separate ways, although I did make sure none of the expense for her treatment was on her shoulders and that she had whatever she needed to get healthy again. Which she managed to do. She sent me a card about six months ago to let me know things were back on track for her. She's engaged to someone else, a mechanic she said no one has ever heard of. She's happy. Living under the radar again and happy. And I'm happy for her. She deserves it."

Cassie could tell he meant that.

"Wow, your story is a lot worse than my story about Brandon and the pigs in a blanket," she said with a hint of humor, hoping to lighten the tone.

"I wasn't trying to one-up you. But you did ask," he said the same way, able to smile again, but a bit wryly.

He stood then and held out a hand to her. "Now that I've put a damper on this wedding for you, let me see what I can do to cheer it up again. Dance with me."

Cassie hadn't even noticed that the band had begun

playing or that Ben and Clair had kicked off that portion of the reception. But not only were her brother and his new wife on the wooden dance floor that had been brought in to cover the lawn, several other couples were there, too.

And she was only too eager to take Joshua up on his offer.

"I just have one more question," she ventured as he swung her onto the dance floor and into his arms.

"Maybe just *one* more," he said facetiously.

"I don't remember anything about your fiancée trying to kill herself in the news. And it seems like it would have been."

"It would have been *big* news. But I went into overdrive keeping it out of the press. I did everything I could to put a lid on it. Bribes, donations, begging, pleading, promises—"

"Extreme measures," she said, recalling something he'd said earlier in the week about everything about him being *out there for public consumption* except what he'd gone to extreme measures to keep quiet.

"Ultimately, though," he added, "what I had to do was agree to give the press and the picture hounds free rein over me for a long time afterward in exchange for burying the story. I had to cooperate with just about everything they wanted and basically sell my soul until Jennie *wasn't* news anymore. And since then I've stuck with women who are used to being in the public eye. Women who actually relish it."

"You say that as if dating models and movie stars has been a terrible burden for you," Cassie teased.

Joshua inclined his head. "You'd be surprised. I'm not wild about vain, shallow, self-centered women who are obsessed with themselves and being seen, and that's how a lot of them are. It's why there haven't been too many repeat dates. And no other real relationships to speak of for over two years now."

He pulled her in closer and whispered in her ear, "Which, maybe, is why I'm enjoying this one enough to let you bring me down with all this ancient history."

He stood straight again and Cassie looked up at him, studying his oh-so-amazing face. "I'm sorry."

"You should be," he pretended to chastise. "You'll just have to make it up to me."

"How?"

His smile was pure, sexy evil. "I don't know. But it's early yet and we have all night to figure it out…"

Chapter Thirteen

It was after midnight before the last of the wedding guests and the bride and groom left the celebration. Cassie, her mother, her brothers and Ad's wife Kit agreed to meet back there the following afternoon to clean up, and then they all said good-night, too.

Reid had a patient he wanted to look in on at the small hospital that served Northbridge's medical needs and since Cassie didn't have her car and he had to go right by her house to get there, he offered to drop off Cassie and take Joshua to the chancellor's cottage. Joshua insisted he could walk to the campus from Cassie's place, that Reid didn't need to go out of his way.

So, by a quarter to one on Saturday morning, Cassie found herself on her porch once again with Joshua.

And it *was* 12:45 a.m.—certainly late enough to call it a night.

But like every other evening she'd been with him this week, she wasn't eager to do that.

Which was why, rather than thanking him for coming to the wedding, she said, "What's on your agenda for the weekend and the end of the Parents' Week events?" And she said it while opening her front door and leading him inside as if it were something they were both accustomed to doing.

"That's kind of up for discussion," he answered, closing the door behind them.

She'd left the light above her kitchen sink on and it provided a little illumination that spilled through the archway that connected the living room and kitchen. Cassie decided against traversing the entire maze of boxes to get to the lamp in the corner, and instead stayed only a few feet inside the door, facing Joshua.

Besides, if she didn't invite him to come any farther in, this was actually just where they'd ended up saying good-night and that sat better with her conscience.

"You and Alyssa are still discussing what to do this weekend?" she asked, telling herself that his plans were something she needed to know because if he was continuing with the remainder of the Parents' Week activities, the dean and the mayor would expect her to go on being his guide.

"Right, Alyssa and I are talking about whether I should stay or not. She's in a few of the performances and exhibitions, but they're repeats of what I've already seen during the week."

"For the parents who could only get here over the weekend," Cassie contributed.

"So she won't be doing anything new and I get the impression that she doesn't want to hurt my feelings, but that given her choice between seeing the new boy-friend this weekend or seeing big brother, she'd opt for the new boyfriend. There's also the issue of parents coming in who I haven't met yet and the increased risk of us—me in particular—being recognized. We've gotten by so far. I'm not sure if we should push our luck."

He stepped nearer, standing within arm's reach of Cassie to lean one shoulder against the wall. She had to raise her chin to look at him. Not that it wasn't worth it, because even in the dim light he looked so terrific she just wanted to go on staring at him. Indefinitely...

But he was talking about leaving town. Soon. And that was something that was just sinking in.

"So, you could be going tomorrow, even?" she heard herself say with much more alarm in her tone than she'd intended.

He took one more step toward her without removing his shoulder from the wall, almost closing the distance between them but not actually making any physical contact.

"If I did leave tomorrow," he said as if he were postulating, "you'd be off the hook. You could have your weekend free, too. To do what you've probably been itching to do all week—unpack."

What she'd been itching for all week was not unpacking.

"Nothing is going anywhere," she said. "It'll all be here for me whenever I get to it, so there's no hurry."

"Does that mean that if I stick around for a couple more days you'll still see me? Even if it doesn't have anything to do with the college?"

"Maybe," she hedged flirtatiously. Then, to contradict that flirtatiousness, she said, "But you're right, not risking any more people seeing you and recognizing either of you has some merit. And you have done the lion's share of Parents' Week. No one could fault you for not staying for the finale."

He glanced around at her disarray, arched an eyebrow and said, "Or…you and I could hide out here and no one would be the wiser. I could help you get through some of this stuff—to pay you back and to make losing all this time up to you."

Cassie had to laugh at that suggestion. "Joshua Cantrell is going to help me unpack moving boxes?"

He grinned and it went instantly to her blood stream to make it run faster. "Sure. It's the least I can do."

"The dean and the mayor would have me run out of town for something like that. You're supposed to be catered to, not put to work. And what kind of a role model would either of us be for Alyssa if you moved in with me for two days?"

Joshua took a breath and sighed it out. "I suppose *that's* true. I guess that leaves me back at square one—maybe taking off tomorrow."

"Or at least on Sunday…" Cassie said, thinking out loud.

"I definitely have to be at a meeting on Monday, so yeah, I guess that's true. It's either tomorrow or Sunday."

"And Alyssa isn't against it being tomorrow," Cassie reminded them both as the wheels of her mind began to spin.

This could very well be her last chance, she thought. Her last chance to be with Joshua. A man unlike any man she'd ever met. A man she was hotter for than any man she'd ever known.

What was she going to do?

Was she going to let him walk out the door and pass up the final opportunity to be with him? Because not only was what had happened between them the night before fresh in her mind, the air around them now was charged enough to let her know that that opportunity was just waiting for her. Inches away…

Was she going to let him walk out the door and never know what it would have been like to have been with him? To give herself over to him and to everything she'd been thinking about, feeling, *itching* for, all week long? And if she did pass up that chance, wouldn't she always wonder what it might have been like? Wouldn't she always wish she'd found out?

Wouldn't she always regret that she hadn't?

Or were the multiple glasses of champagne she'd had throughout the reception clouding her judgment?

After all, she *hadn't* had as much to drink the night before and she'd stopped them from doing what it had seemed like they shouldn't do….

But what *had* stopped her the night before? she asked herself as she stared at his white shirt and tie and suffered the almost intolerable desire to grab that tie and pull him to her.

What had stopped her the night before had been her sheets. And remembering that they hadn't been good enough for Brandon. That eventually, in his opinion, neither had she. That eventually Joshua might come to the same conclusion.

But it occurred to her suddenly that there wasn't an *eventually* when it came to Joshua. There was possibly—probably—only tonight….

"You're not really here with me anymore, are you? Mentally, at least," she heard Joshua say through the distraction of her thoughts.

She glanced at his face again. "I wasn't. But I'm back."

"Where'd you go?"

She smiled. "Down the path of rationalization."

That made him smile, too. As if he knew what that rationalization had been about. But he asked anyway. "What were you rationalizing?"

"This."

"This?"

"Your being here now. And maybe not later…"

"So maybe we should seize the moment?" he guessed.

"Is there a moment to seize?" she countered.

He laughed a wry, devilish laugh. "Oh, yeah." He snapped his fingers. "About that quick there could be a moment. I'm just trying not to do what you shied away from doing last night."

"And if I wasn't so shy tonight?" she asked in a very quiet voice.

The smile he flashed at her then was wicked and so, so sexy before he snapped his fingers a second time. "I'll try not to be that quick. But I want you so damn bad I can't make any promises."

It was Cassie's turn to laugh. "Now there's a selling point if ever I've heard one," she joked.

Joshua leaned forward and kissed her, his lips parted and just moist enough, just firm enough, just inviting enough.

"How about this?" he said when he'd ended it. "If you'll let me see what's beyond these boxes, I'll make your favorite breakfast in the morning."

"You know how to make my mom's apple waffles?"

"I can call her and find out."

"Oh good, another big selling point—calling my mother to tell her I let you spend the night."

Joshua kissed her again and she wondered if he knew that each kiss was a selling point all its own.

"*Are* you letting me spend the night?"

"Maybe," she repeated.

He reached a single index finger up to brush her bangs away from her eye, trailing that finger along the side of her face and into one of her dimples before it ended up under her chin to raise it so he could kiss her again. This time with his lips parted still more.

But once that kiss was over, Cassie could see he wasn't kidding around anymore. His expression had sobered. "Don't tease me, Cassie. I want you too much."

That was when she made her decision. Looking up into his silver-gray eyes, bathed in the warmth of them, she saw a raw desire that mirrored what she realized she was feeling. She saw, too, the man inside, a man who could be as vulnerable as she was. And she knew that no matter what came after that moment, she wanted tonight with him, too. She wanted him.

"I don't have fancy sheets," she warned.

He laughed again. "I don't care what kind of sheets you have."

It was the right answer. Cassie did what she'd been thinking about doing a bit earlier—she reached out and took his tie in hand, using it to tug him behind her when she turned and walked out of the living room, down the hall and to her bedroom.

Once she had Joshua there she released his tie and made her way through the pitch blackness to her night-stand to light a candle she burned when she read at night before going to sleep. Then she turned, finding that Joshua had removed his suit coat, tie, shoes and socks, and was in the process of pulling his shirttails from his slacks.

Now that she'd come this far, Cassie suffered a lapse in courage and stayed where she was, beside the bed.

Joshua apparently felt no timidity because he crossed to her, unbuttoning his shirt as he did and exposing— inch by inch—a chest and six-pack abs that made Cassie go breathless.

And in her initial awe of that body she'd only imag-ined, that body that was hard and cut and better than even the best images she'd come up with in her fanta-sies, she could only think to step out of her shoes and kick them away.

With his hands on the last and lowest button, Joshua leaned in to kiss her again.

That she was becoming familiar with and Cassie

sought the comfort and confidence of that familiarity, closing her eyes, parting her own lips, meeting his tongue as it came to say hi.

When he was finished with his shirt buttons he cupped her face with both hands, holding her to the kiss she had no inclination to escape from, the kiss that was eager and sensual.

So sensual that it infused Cassie with renewed boldness and she let her hands sneak up inside his shirtfront, laying her palms flat against his chest.

Warm, satin-over-marble hard muscle—that was what she indulged in, kneading, massaging, not realizing until after the fact that she was doing to his pectorals what her breasts were beginning to long for.

But Joshua had other things in mind for her. Like opening his mouth even wider to intensify that kiss, and abandoning her face to wrap his arms around her, to press his hands firmly to her back, to do some massaging himself before he unzipped her dress.

He wasted no time trailing his hands up and over her shoulders then, urging the wide V to spread, to fall down her arms until the rest of the dress went with it to land in a filmy circle around her feet.

Black strapless bra. Black lace bikini panties. Thigh-high hose. That was what Cassie was left in. That was what Joshua stopped kissing her to look at.

"Oh, yeah…" he breathed, part groan, part sigh, all approval, admiration and arousal as he dipped down to kiss her left breast where it bulged above the tight bra.

That sent bright, sparkling little glitters of delight all through her and took her to a new level of wanting him.

But Cassie sent his shirt on the same journey her dress had made and paid more attention to getting her own full glimpse of his naked torso than to her exposure or the fact that within the cups of that bra her nipples had become tiny, supersensitive pebbles.

And it was worth it. Because there in front of her, beneath hands that could now touch it all, were broad, broad shoulders that somehow looked more massive without clothes than they had within them. There were pectorals that looked as wonderful as they felt. There was a narrow waist and even a navel that was sexier than she'd ever thought a navel could be, above a thin line of hair that disappeared behind the waistband of his pants.

Pants she wasn't going to allow to block her view, either.

She reached for the hidden hook above the zipper and unhinged it. Then she went for the zipper itself, feeling the more than substantial ridge behind it that proved Joshua really did want her. As much as he'd said he did.

He chuckled. "Give me a second," he said in a voice that had grown guttural, reaching into his pocket to retrieve condoms before he gave the go-ahead and Cassie dropped his drawers.

Well, not all of his drawers. He may have brought protection just in case, but he'd still worn shorts—boxers that made Cassie smile because they seemed so ordinary.

That was as far as she got in undressing him, though, because he recaptured her mouth with his, sending his tongue to plunder as he reached around and unfastened her bra.

Her nipples went from pebbles to sharp shards of

diamonds that met both his palms when they came to cover them. To caress. To squeeze. To lift and press and work into a frenzy of need for even more.

A frenzy of need that was left unmet as Joshua eased Cassie back onto the bed then, divesting himself of those ordinary boxer shorts.

But what awaited her when they were gone was anything but ordinary.

He was awesome.

But she caught just a brief look before he joined her on the bed and took one of her breasts into his mouth.

It felt so amazing, it answered so strong a craving in her, that Cassie could only lie back and revel in that for a while. And when she yearned for more of him, it was her hands and her own mouth that did the exploring.

Long, lean, lithe. Hard and honed. Tight and taut. There was nothing about him that didn't turn her on. That didn't increase her will for more. Cassie savored it all, vacillating between the wonders of what she was discovering of him and the wonders he was bestowing on her as he left not even an inch of her without the attention of lips and tongue and magic, magic hands that began to work her into a frenzy, releasing in them both something wild and primal and shouting to have its due.

Something that couldn't be, that wouldn't be, contained. That grew and grew and pulsed with a life of its own until it was more powerful than either of them.

Safely sheathed, Joshua came above Cassie then and she didn't hesitate to open herself to him, to make way for that oh-so-extraordinary part of him to find a home inside of her.

Hot, slippery, smooth, he glided into her, urging her with his hands to wrap her legs around his hips. It all felt so incredible that Cassie's spine arched in response, pulling her up off the mattress to meet him, to move with him. Hips flexed against hips as he thrust into her, as she thrust towards him, as they both retreated to do it again. And again. And again.

Speed quickened. Every sensation intensified. Need mounted, expanded, swelled within Cassie until it overwhelmed her, controlled her and finally exploded into something brighter than bright, blinding her, immobilizing her, holding her within its grasp while wave after wave rippled through her, rocked her and then left her limp with pleasure. Pleasure frosted by Joshua reaching his own summit, tensing, freezing, plunging more deeply into her than she would have ever thought possible, culminating with a dark, husky groan that rumbled from his throat when he, too, climaxed.

Then everything stilled.

Bodies eased. Energy ebbed. Breathing began again from lungs that had held air prisoner. And all was quiet as that bliss settled and they melded together like two slabs of hot, pliable clay in perfect symmetry against each other.

Only after a time of that exquisite peace did Joshua's passion-ravaged voice interrupt the silence.

"I saw it in the dimples the first time I laid eyes on you."

"What did you see in my dimples?" Cassie asked, her chin in the curve of his shoulder, staring up at the play of candlelight on her ceiling while he was facedown, the side of his forehead pressed to the side of hers.

"The dimples told me it would be like this—mind-blowing."

Joshua pushed himself up enough to look down at her. To study her face as if there were something there he needed to read.

He smiled and Cassie felt too good not to smile, too.

Which was when he grinned. "Yep, there they are. Killer dimples. Hiding out here in Small Town, Montana—a secret weapon."

He kissed first one of her dimples, then the other, and when Cassie could see his handsome features again, they'd smoothed into an expression that was more contemplative, caring, tender.

"Convince me that you're unhurt, unscathed and unremorseful," he ordered.

Cassie pushed her hips up into his where their bodies were still united. "All of the above," she assured.

She wasn't sure whether it was the hip action or the assurance or both, but something made him grin again before he rolled to his back and pulled her close against his side. "Then I can rest up."

"For…"

He smiled that wicked smile she'd seen earlier and closed his eyes. "The phone call to your mom for the pancake recipe."

"It's waffles. Apple waffles."

He laughed. "Waffles. Apple waffles. And then we'll unpack boxes and say to hell with being a good role model and I may never leave here again," he said, his voice drifting off and letting her know he was, too.

But even though Cassie was heavy with fatigue herself, she wasn't as quick to sleep. Not when she couldn't help wondering if he really meant what he'd just said.

If he actually did intend to stick around.

And if that was as good an idea as it seemed at that moment.

Because at that moment, when she was so completely satiated and happy, it seemed like the greatest idea she'd ever heard.

Chapter Fourteen

Joshua woke up Saturday morning before Cassie did. Brilliant sunshine flooded through her as-yet-curtainless window in a glorious early autumn day.

But he didn't lounge in the heat of the sun patch that fell across the blanket that covered them both. He slipped out of bed. He'd promised her breakfast and he intended to honor that promise. Not with waffles—apple or otherwise—but he figured he could at least scramble eggs or something. And serve it to her in bed, where she was still sleeping with her russet-colored hair all tousled against her pillow, and her long eyelashes resting against high, naturally pink cheekbones that added up to that girl-next-door look he just couldn't get enough of.

He pulled on only his shorts and quietly padded out

of the small bedroom that was littered with half a dozen unpacked boxes, going to the kitchen that, like the living room, was full of them. They were stacked on the floor, on the countertops, on the small kitchen table and even on the seats of the four chairs that surrounded it. There was a microwave oven already set up, though, and as long as there was that, he knew he could cook eggs.

If there were any.

He opened the refrigerator and discovered that while it was mostly unstocked, there *was* a carton of eggs along with some milk and a brick of cheese he could use.

He took it all out, kicked the door closed and then found a spot of clear counter space on which to deposit them before he went in search of a bowl.

The cupboards held only a few coffee mugs and a bag of ground coffee. He recognized that it was his fault that Cassie hadn't gotten anything put away this week, but was grateful nonetheless for that discovery. Before he continued the exploration for plates, bowls and utensils, he stopped to make coffee in the coffeemaker near the sink.

Then he returned to his previous quest.

After snooping through several boxes of pots, pans, glasses and assorted kitchen things, he located two boxes that held what he needed.

"Bingo!" he muttered to himself, thinking that he was going to be able to make this work after all.

And that got him to thinking.

Maybe he could make everything with Cassie work…

It was amazing how much that notion appealed to

him. As much as Cassie herself did. So much that as he cracked eggs and sliced the cheese, his mind began to wander to what making everything with Cassie work might actually mean.

Having a full-blown relationship with her. A future with her. A life with her. Having Cassie with him. Being with her here, in Northbridge. With her family and friends. In this small, friendly town that had made him feel welcome this last week for no reason other than that that was how they treated people.

It definitely had an appeal. A strong one. And as the appeal took over, it sprouted roots and grew.

He thought about having Cassie to come home to at the end of every day, picturing that taking place in L.A. where he lived most of the time. He thought about having his evenings with her—going to the movies, to the charity dinners and sporting events, and all the other things that took up a lot of those evenings. He thought about spending some of them home alone with her, realizing that even doing something as mundane as watching television had a whole new glow to it when he put Cassie in the picture.

He thought about taking her with him to the apartment he kept in New York for the three or four months a year he spent there.

"Cassie in New York," he said softly to himself as if it were the title of a book as he scooped the cut-up cheese into the eggs and added milk to the mix.

He liked the mental image of the small-town girl in the heart of that city. The fantasy of showing it to her. Of taking her shopping. Of giving her the grand tour. Of club-hopping. Of sharing pizza and pasta with her at the little hole-in-the-wall Italian restaurant he made sure he went to at least once a week whenever he was there.

And from New York he envisioned them going to Paris, to London, to Switzerland. To all the places where he vacationed or visited friends or went for business or to just get away. And every bit of it had an entirely new allure when he thought of being there with her.

As he began the initial strokes of beating the eggs, he thought about having her to come home to wherever he was. He thought about having her to go to bed with every night, no matter where he was. He thought about having her to wake up with every morning. And just imagining it gave him a warm rush.

He didn't have a single doubt that he would like knowing that he would be able to see her each and every day. To see that face, those dimples. That each and every day he'd be able to hear that voice, that laugh. That he'd be able to reach out and touch her, hold her hand, put his arm around her. Take her to bed...

He beat the eggs harder and faster just picturing it.

Cassie in his life. Filling it. Completing it. Making it real. The way she had this last week. But not just here and now. Here and now and everywhere else. Forever.

It would be great....

He took the eggs to the microwave, figured out how to work it and then began the cooking process, crossing his arms over his bare middle and leaning against the counter's edge to wait.

It really would be great, he went on musing. Great not to leave Northbridge without her. Not to get on his motorcycle and have nothing left of her but memories. Not to have to miss her the way he already knew he would. Not to have her be only this brief interlude. Not to have it end at all.

And not only would that mean having Cassie with him, it would also mean having a little hint of North-bridge with him, as well.

That had an attraction, too.

What had Alyssa said when they'd talked about Northbridge early in the week? Something about the people here being so regular, so normal?

It occurred to Joshua that that was yet another thing that having Cassie in his life would bring—a hint of Northbridge and a sense of normalcy. A grounding force. And a breath of fresh air to go with everything else she had to offer.

The microwave went off and he turned to retrieve the eggs, feeling something well up inside him that he hadn't felt in a long, long time. Something that felt right. Something that felt *just* right. Perfect, in fact...

Cassie...

"Joshua? Are you somewhere?" she said from the bedroom as if his thoughts had somehow called out to her.

And the simple sound of her sleepy voice made him grin so broadly it almost hurt his cheeks. Even if her tone was tentative and unsure and maybe slightly worried. Maybe worried that he'd left her high and dry, as though she were nothing more than a one-night stand.

But Cassie wasn't a one-night stand. She was so much more....

"Stay there," he commanded, feeling full of hope that he really could do this. That he could have Cassie and a whole lifetime with her...

There was one box he recalled coming across in his search that held only a few pantry items. He found it again, grabbed it and emptied it in a hurry. Upturning it to use as a tray, he placed a single plate piled with the eggs that they could share, two forks and two cups of coffee on it.

Then he took it with him out of the kitchen, wondering as he retraced his steps down the hall just how bad cold eggs tasted. Because at that moment he was craving Cassie and being back in bed with her more than food...

When he got to the bedroom she was sitting up against the headboard, knees bent in front of her, holding the sheet tightly over her breasts, a pillow crease marking one side of her face, and wide, unaccented eyes waiting to catch sight of him.

And that was when Joshua hesitated.

She looked stop-in-his-tracks beautiful to him. As golden bright as the day itself. And right there in that bright, beautiful face was reflected everything that had gotten to him since he'd met her: that she was soft, sweet, kind, caring, giving, funny, honest, selfless, unassuming and totally unaware of just how incredible she was. Everything he wanted.

But she also looked so open, so vulnerable, so unguarded.

So not what he'd had to become accustomed to since Jennie.

So what he couldn't have.

And that was when reality threw a bucket of ice water on him.

"Oh, I must look awful!" Cassie said, interpreting the change that overtook Joshua's expression almost the instant he came into the bedroom and saw her.

"Just the opposite," he said as if he meant it. "You look like exactly what I want to wrap my arms around and never let go of."

That made her smile but, still suffering a bout of self-consciousness, she held on to the sheet with her elbows, dipped her head down and ran her fingers through her hair to comb it in a makeshift fashion.

Joshua crossed to the side of the bed that he'd spent the night on and set the cardboard box he was carrying on the mattress.

"See? I told you I'd fix you breakfast."

"You told me you'd fix my *favorite* breakfast," she amended.

"I think you were just hearing things," he countered with a smile of his own that went a long way in reassuring her that she wasn't *too* repulsive, even though she'd opened her eyes only a few minutes earlier.

But that reassurance waned suddenly because rather than rejoining her on the bed for breakfast, he went to get his suit pants and put them on.

"Are you leaving?" she asked before considering that it might sound desperate or clingy.

With his pants on and then his shirt, too—albeit un-buttoned and untucked—he came again to the bed, this time sitting on it, facing her, but with one foot remaining firmly planted on the floor. And his smile was gone again, replaced by that solemnity that had appeared at the doorway.

"Yeah, I think I have to go. Today. Now," he said quietly.

Just as quietly Cassie said, "But you brought two forks and two cups of coffee…"

"I was going to share the eggs. But I've kind of lost my appetite all of a sudden."

I must look horrible….

"It's weird," he said. "When I brought that stuff in here I was ready to whisk you away to a whole life of us being together—"

"And then you saw how I look in the morning and—"

"You look… You look good enough for this to be the hardest thing I've ever done, Cassie," he said as if he actually were in some kind of pain. Which again made her believe him, she just didn't understand what was going on.

He reached over and pressed the backs of his fingers to her cheek in a tender caress, staring at her as if he were memorizing her features when he dropped that hand to her upraised knee to squeeze it tight.

"I want you," he said, once more in a faraway, quiet voice. "I wanted you and I to be together. To have a future together. I wanted to take you with me to L.A., to New York, to Paris, everywhere. I wanted to be here in Northbridge with you. With your family. And I walked into this room thinking that maybe I could actually have that. But then I saw you. I remembered who you are. What you are and—"

"Who and what am I," she repeated, instantly afraid that she was reliving what she'd gone through once already in her life. With Brandon.

"Yes, who and what you are," Joshua confirmed. "And no, I'm not thinking bumpkin," he added as if he could read her mind. "Because *bumpkin* is not what you are. What you are is someone who isn't shallow or self-centered or vain, someone who doesn't need or want to be the center of attention, in the limelight. What you are is the real deal. Genuine and..." He shook his head. "Genuine and wonderful and I'm crazy about you."

He paused and she wasn't sure if it was just to give his next words more impact or if it only seemed that way to her.

"Which is why I can't inflict what comes with me on you."

Cassie dropped her face into the sheet that was tented over her knees, as if not looking at him would stop him from saying what he was saying.

It didn't, though.

"I'm a can opener, Cassie. I'm the can opener that opens cans of worms for people who don't deserve to have that happen to them. For people like you. Like your family—"

"Like Jennie," she finished for him, raising her head from her knees to look at him again.

"Yes. Like Jennie. That's what I saw when I came in here. I saw the person I want to be with, who also happens to be someone who could be messed up beyond repair just *because* I want her and she might not make good copy for trashy newspapers and magazines. Someone who would be great to have in my sister's life, too. Someone who Alyssa would get attached to, before we both have to watch her be publicly eviscerated to *make* her good copy. What I saw was everything that happened before—like a flashback—only with you at the center of it. And I knew I couldn't do that to you. Not to you…"

"What could they say about me?" Cassie asked, slightly dazed by the conflicting messages he was giving.

"What *wouldn't* they say about you is the point. They'll say anything. Dig up anything. Make up anything."

"Maybe I could take it." Maybe she could take a whole lot if it meant being with him…

"You say that now, but you don't have any idea what it's like. Flashbulbs blinding you. Rude, intrusive, personal questions shouted at you. Ugly name-calling to see if it'll get a rise out of you. Finding pictures of yourself—pictures you had no idea were being taken that make you look bad—finding them at every checkout counter you go through. Private times invaded as if you don't have a right to them." He sighed in disgust. "Look what I've had to do just to see my sister this week. And it doesn't even guarantee that tomorrow or the next day or next week or next month someone won't realize who she is and ruin this for her. It's its own special kind of hell."

"Worse than growing up with four brothers?" she half joked because she didn't know what to say and was afraid anything else might sound as if she were pleading for him not to be doing this. Certainly not for reasons that didn't seem altogether valid to her if he honestly felt about her the way he'd said.

"Okay, let's talk about those brothers," Joshua said as if accepting a challenge, taking his hand from her knee and putting it on the bed near his own thigh now. Not touching her at all, as if putting that subtle distance between them. "Let's talk about what happens when somebody digs up Ben's troubled teenage years. That's something the tabloids would love to use to drag you and your family through the mud. To say that your mom was abusive or neglectful or worse. To say that your other brothers terrorized him or that the whole lot of them were adolescent criminals who masterminded the car theft. To say things you can't even imagine being said."

Cassie was feeling less and less lighthearted with every word that came out of that mouth she was still craving over her own.

"I told you before, Ben has never kept his problems as a kid a secret. Ridiculous lies aren't going to—"

"You'd be surprised what ridiculous lies can do. They can do damage that snowballs. That harms you and him and his wife. The stress could even harm that baby they'll have in a few months. That baby that could end up being called my *love child* just because your new sister-in-law and I end up at one of your family's backyard barbecues at the same time. And then what? What if even ridiculous lies do cause harm? You'd know that your being with me was the underlying reason for it and you'd feel guilty and angry and responsible, and that would cause *you* harm. Like I said, a can of worms."

Cassie considered what he was saying. She recalled what he'd told her about his former fiancée. She knew that experience had been nearly as traumatic for both Joshua and Alyssa as it had been for Jennie. She knew it had been bad enough for Joshua to feel so guilty that he'd altered his own personal life and who he'd dated ever since.

But what if, another part of her mused, what if that wasn't *all* there was to this now? What if that past experience also gave him a handy excuse? A good way out of something that had only been a little vacation diversion for him with someone he'd known from the start—or at least realized as time had gone by—would never fit into his world any more than she would have fit into Brandon's?

Because Cassie thought that that was certainly a possibility. Especially since he was using it to pave his path out her door rather than presenting it to her as something to consider if she wanted to be involved with him. Something that, it seemed to her, should be her choice. Her decision as to whether or not to put herself in that position. Unless Joshua really just didn't want her. And was too nice to say it outright the way Brandon had.

"Last night shouldn't have happened," she said, more to herself than to him.

"Don't say that. I mean, maybe it shouldn't have, but I can't be sorry that it did. And I sure as hell don't want you to be. I just… I don't know. When I orchestrate getaways like this, I have the chance to be removed from what it's like the rest of the time. I get to forget some things. Like what comes with being who I am. I let down my guard. I guess that's why this went as far as it did even though I knew better. That and that…" His eyes met hers and he looked deeply into them. "That I couldn't help myself when it came to you. I honestly…care about you."

Or had he just played her? Was he just playing her now?

Cassie hated that that occurred to her, but it did.

And if that was the case, if he *had* played her, if he *was* playing her, she wasn't going to let him see that he'd gotten to her. That this was anything more to her than it was to him.

So she shrugged as if it wasn't.

"It's okay. I knew that last night was just what it was. It was one night together before you left and I never saw you again. And it really is okay," she repeated even though it didn't feel at all okay. "Last night was fun, we had a good time, now you can take off. No hard feelings," she ended with a lie.

"Come on—that's not you talking. And that isn't how things have been between us, either—some kind of superficial fooling around. We *connected*."

"And now we're disconnecting."

"Just like that?" he said, sounding as if he were on the verge of anger.

But anger was better than what she was feeling.

"Just like that," Cassie confirmed with finality, wishing he would leave before she lost the cool, aloof facade she was hiding behind.

"This isn't right," he said then, suspicious, maybe, of how she was handling it.

But along with the raw hurt that was rapidly taking hold of her, Cassie was furious with herself. Furious for doing this a second time, for putting herself in this position again. And she was not going to degrade herself by showing him more than she already had.

"This was just a week out of our lives, Joshua. Lives we both need to get back to now—yours out there in the world with photographers and reporters watching, and mine here in Northbridge. So let's just say it's been fun and do that."

"It's been more than that," he insisted. "And I want you—I *need* you—to know that I'm not doing this for any reason except that I believe it's what's best for you."

Cassie managed another shrug. "Okay. It's been more than just fun. But now it's over, so there's no reason to drag it out. You *should* leave today, the way you said earlier. You should leave now, in fact. You should go find Alyssa, say your goodbyes to her and leave town."

"Cassie…"

He reached a hand to take her knee again and she swiveled away before he could, finishing what she had to say. "Then I'll forget I ever knew you. You can forget you ever knew me, and we'll both get on with it."

"I'm not going to forget I knew you. It would probably be easier if I could."

"I'm sure you'll find a way," she said under her breath. Then, as the tears she was fighting threatened almost unbearably, she said, "Really. Go."

He didn't, though. Not right away. He stayed sitting there for a moment, watching her until Cassie thought she couldn't hold out anymore and would break down in front of him.

But just when she was on the verge of that, he finally

stood and Cassie's gaze followed that glorious torso peeking at her from between the open edges of his shirt all the way up to that face it hurt so much to look at now.

"I don't know what else to say," he said softly. "I'm sorry. I hate that it has to be this way. But for your own good—"

"I know. I got it. Thanks. Now go ahead and go," she said, sounding less in control because she *was* less in control. Because those controls that had brought her this far were slipping.

But he finally did as she'd been telling him to—he gathered the rest of his things and walked out of the room.

Cassie pinched her eyes shut so tightly they ached and held her breath, listening to his footfalls down the hallway and to the front door.

But he didn't go out right then.

She waited. She listened. A part of her hoped he wouldn't go at all, that he would come back and somehow make everything that had just gone on go away instead....

Then she heard her front door open and she realized he must have just finished dressing in her entryway before he left.

But he did leave. Closing the door quietly, securely behind him.

And that was when Cassie dropped her head to her knees yet again, hugged them hard with both arms and let the tears have their day.

Chapter Fifteen

"What's going on around here?" Cassie asked.

Two weeks had passed since she'd spent the night with Joshua and he'd left town. She hadn't heard a word from him, and she hadn't seen his sister around campus, either—even though she'd checked and knew that Alyssa was still attending the college.

Cassie had assumed the younger woman was avoiding her and so had been surprised by a phone call from her early that Friday morning. Alyssa wanted Cassie to meet her for coffee that afternoon at Adz. Cassie also assumed that because the college student hadn't merely come to her office, this must not be about something to do with Alyssa's classes. But still she'd agreed. Without having any of her curiosity about why Alyssa wanted to meet with her satisfied ahead of time.

Only suddenly Cassie's curiosity regarding something else entirely had been aroused. So when she went into her brother's restaurant and discovered that Alyssa wasn't there yet, but that Ad, Reid and Luke were talking as intently as several other groups of people she'd come across along Main Street, she went directly to the end of the big, carved wood bar where her brothers were huddled and asked her question, adding, "The whole town is buzzing and now it looks like you guys are, too."

"They found something at the bridge," Reid answered when she joined them. "Luke and the rest of the police force were out there all morning."

"What did you find, a body?" Cassie asked facetiously, thinking that that was preposterous.

"No, we didn't find a body. But we did find something that's making us wonder if we better start looking for one," Luke said. "The men working on remodeling the bridge found an old duffel bag stuffed up in the rafters."

"An old duffel bag," Cassie echoed.

"It looks like it belonged to one of the two men who robbed the bank back in 1960 with Reverend Perry's wife."

That did pique Cassie's interest, something that hadn't happened since Joshua had left and all she'd been able to think about—obsess over—was him.

But the bank robbery of 1960 was one of the biggest things that had ever happened in Northbridge.

Two migrant workers had come into town that autumn for the harvest. Transient farmhands could be a good lot or a bad one, and according to the stories that had been told ever since, those two were bad from the start. Loud, crude, hard-drinking, hell-raising troublemakers whom everyone in Northbridge had been eager to see move on at the end of the harvest.

Everyone except the wife of the man who had been the church's minister at the time.

It had been well known that Celeste Perry was feeling stifled and unfulfilled as wife, mother of two sons and female example of the kind of righteousness her husband preached about every Sunday. But no one had expected her to take up with the likes of the two bad-news farmhands.

And even when the worst of the rumors were flying about late nights she'd been seen out with the men, no one would have ever predicted that from that, the bank would be robbed and Celeste and the two men would disappear with the money.

So it was no wonder a discovery—the first discovery of anything linked to the crime or the people who were believed to have committed it—was huge news in Northbridge.

"What was in the duffel bag?" Cassie asked her police officer brother.

"Looks like the clothes and belongings of one of the farmhands," Luke said. "And the empty money bags from the bank. There also seems to be a stain on the outside of the bag that could be blood. Reid's going to test it for us to make sure."

"So what's the thinking? That the reverend's wife and one of the men killed the other man?"

Luke shrugged, but the arch of his eyebrows told her that scenario was certainly being considered. "Better to do a two-way split than a three-way," Luke said. "Plus, a man and a woman traveling together looks a lot less suspicious than a woman traveling with two men— which was what state troopers and the sheriff's department and the state police and the local guys were all searching for and asking questions about at the time."

"Then you really are going to start looking for a body?" Cassie asked, amazed that such a thing could happen in Northbridge.

"Could be," Luke answered. "Especially if Reid tests that stain and tells us it's human blood. Time will tell."

Luke stood up from the barstool he'd been perched atop. "I'd better get back. So, Ad, you'll let your co-horts on the town council know that we're stopping work on the bridge and treating it like a crime scene for now, right?"

"I will," Ad confirmed.

"And Reid," Luke said then, "we'll have that duffel over to the hospital in an hour or so."

Alyssa Cantrell came into the restaurant as Reid assured Luke that he was headed back to the hospital as soon as he finished his hamburger.

Cassie cast the college student a smile and just that quickly even big local news paled and thoughts of Joshua shined bright, hot and painful again in her mind.

"This is actually the reason I came in," she said quietly to her brothers, who both glanced at Alyssa.

The eighteen-year-old didn't seem to notice anyone but Cassie, though, as she crossed to her with a tenuous, nervous-looking smile of her own.

"Hi. Thanks for meeting me," Alyssa said when she reached Cassie.

"It's good to see you," Cassie told her.

She introduced her brothers before Luke left, ordered two coffees from Ad and then took a small booth near the bar.

"How are you? Any problems with your classes or anything?" Cassie asked to get the ball rolling because now that Alyssa had her there, she didn't seem to know where to begin.

"I'm good and so are all my classes," Alyssa responded, fiddling with the strap on her wristwatch. "I s'pose you thought it was weird when I called," she said then.

"No, not weird," Cassie lied. "I was glad you did. I *am* still your adviser. And a friend, too, I hope."

"This isn't about school. Or me," Alyssa said as if she wanted to get that out of the way completely. "This is about Joshua. And you."

It hadn't occurred to Cassie before that moment that Alyssa might have wanted to meet with her to tell her off. To voice some sort of disapproval or dislike or disgust. To tell her she'd had no business getting involved with Joshua. To call her names. But suddenly all of those possibilities flashed through her head and she wondered if this was going to be unpleasant.

But then Alyssa said, "Joshua has been really, really unhappy since he left here."

"So has she."

Cassie's back was to her brothers, but she knew it was Reid who had interjected that comment.

And to make matters worse, Ad brought their coffee in time to say, "Unhappy is an understatement. She's miserable."

"Thanks, guys," Cassie said sarcastically.

Although the truth was that she'd been so unhappy, so miserable that she'd even broken down and confided to her family who Joshua and Alyssa actually were and that she'd fallen for Joshua only to have him leave her as high and dry as Brandon had.

The trouble was, despite the fact that she'd known her family would never reveal the Cantrells' identities to anyone, she hadn't bargained on them liking Joshua more than they had Brandon and trying to convince her to do something to get Joshua back into her life.

"Maybe we should move," Cassie suggested to Alyssa then, not having thought before that they were sitting within hearing range of her brothers.

But for some reason, Alyssa didn't seem to care about privacy. "That's okay. I'm not going to say anything I shouldn't. I just wanted to tell you… Well, I know some of the reason Joshua broke up with you was my fault and I'm sorry."

Sorry or not, it didn't make Cassie feel one whit less awful than she had since the moment Joshua had walked out her front door.

Still, Cassie said, "It's okay."

"No, I don't think it's okay," Alyssa insisted. "I feel guilty. My brother has sacrificed a lot for me and even though things have worked out for the most part, his leaving you and being as sad as he's been—because of me—has bothered me. I haven't been able to eat or sleep or study—it's weighing on me."

"You were a factor, Alyssa, but you weren't the biggest factor," Cassie said, because she didn't see anything to be gained by this girl suffering for what Cassie was convinced would have happened anyway. The bottom line was that Joshua could have caviar on toast points whenever he wanted. But Cassie was peanut butter on soda crackers. And while peanut butter on soda crackers might taste good occasionally, when a person could have the caviar on toast points as a steady diet, they weren't going to settle for the peanut butter.

"I know what the biggest factor was," Alyssa said with a glance in the direction of Ad and Reid. "But I've done some thinking—and talking to a psychologist I saw a while ago—and I've started to believe that Joshua and I were both wrong. I called him and told him so last night, and that's why I wanted to see you today. I don't want to be the blame for you not getting together. Or for my brother to be as mopey as he's been for the last two weeks. Or for him not having what he wants if he wants you."

If...

That seemed like an enormous *if* to Cassie and the biggest factor, even if Alyssa believed it was the issue of the tabloids hounding Cassie and hurting her feelings in print.

"See, the thing is this," Alyssa said, "I thought that because you were from Northbridge and not very... Don't take this wrong, but I thought that maybe you weren't very *worldly* or something—"

"I know what you mean and I'm not taking it wrong," Cassie assured her.

"I thought that that made you like Jennie. But I asked around and I got Joshua to tell me some things about you, and I talked to my old therapist on the phone, and

I finally figured out that you and Jennie might not be so much the same. I liked Jennie, she got to be sort of the sister I'd never had. But she was… I don't want to say she was weak or anything. But she wasn't very strong. Or tough. Or resilient. She took everything really hard and she had…"

Alyssa was obviously having difficulty with this but Cassie didn't know how to help her out, so she waited for Alyssa to find the words.

When she did, the younger woman went on. "Joshua and I have had bad things happen in our lives, and I know so have you. Well, Jennie had hard times in her life, too. But you know how that kind of stuff becomes a part of you, but how you still have to learn to let go of some of it so when you get reminded of it, it can't wipe you out all over again?"

"Yes."

"Jennie couldn't do that. It was like it didn't take anything at all to remind her of the bad that had happened and once she'd been reminded, she couldn't get over it again without going through some whole grieving process and reliving it, and suffering all over as if it was new."

"Some people have problems like that," Cassie said kindly.

"I guess she just feels things too deeply and maybe that's why they stick with her. But it wasn't only the big deals or what had happened a long time ago, it was new things, too. Small things. Even if they were just lies that you're better off ignoring. Jennie couldn't ignore *any-*

thing. And then she couldn't handle it, either. She took it all inside and let it eat at her."

Cassie nodded in understanding.

"But from what I've heard, that doesn't sound like you," Alyssa said.

"I can't say I don't feel things deeply," Cassie said because she didn't know what Alyssa had been told, but she couldn't have her thinking that she was some sort of superwoman.

"But it seems like you know what to take seriously and what to just blow off, too. And Jennie could never figure that out or couldn't blow off anything even if we told her that was something *to* blow off. I mean, I'm not saying that some really mean stuff didn't get thrown at her because of Joshua. Or that it wouldn't get thrown at you, if you were with him, because it might. I'm just saying that sometimes it seemed like Jennie could have ignored some things, but she never did. She couldn't. Or wouldn't, I'm not sure which. And maybe you could. And would. Which is what I told my brother last night."

"What did he think about that?" Cassie asked, hating that she could hardly take a breath until she heard the answer, hating that she was having difficulty remembering that the tabloid problem wasn't the only problem she honestly believed existed.

"Joshua didn't tell me *what* he thought about my theory," Alyssa answered, unaware of Cassie's internal turmoil. "He just said he'd think about it. But I told him that I'm giving you my stamp of approval, for what it's worth, and that he shouldn't keep away from you because of me at all."

Cassie nodded slowly, ruminatively, unsure how to respond to that. "Okay. Thank you."

Alyssa hesitated a moment and then said, "But what I think is that you should go and talk to him."

"Is he here in town again?"

Ohhh, she wished that hadn't come out the way it had—fast, eager, hopeful, as if she were wearing her heart on her sleeve….

"No, he's at the L.A. house. But it's Friday and you have the weekend off. You could get there tonight still. And maybe the two of you could talk and figure it out without me as a part of it now."

It seemed apparent that Alyssa was urging Cassie to go to Joshua to soothe her own sense of guilt, not because Joshua had given any indication that that was what he wanted.

And because of that, Cassie hedged. "I don't know if that's such a good idea—"

"I think it's a great idea," Reid chimed in. "In fact, if I didn't have to deal with this duffel bag thing, I'd drive you into Billings myself to catch the next plane to California. But I'll bet Ad, here, would do it, wouldn't you?"

"I would."

Cassie shook her head vehemently. "Yeah. No. I just—"

"I know he'd be glad to see you," Alyssa encouraged. "You should surprise him. I won't even call and warn him that you're coming. I can tell you how to get onto the grounds without setting off security." The young girl smiled mischievously. "I used to do it to sneak out now and then after curfew and then sneak back in later on."

"That just doesn't seem like a good idea," Cassie reiterated, forcing herself to remember her own sense of Joshua's rejection of her being more about her not being in his league than about whether she could handle the scrutiny of a negative press that preferred someone flashier for the Tennis Shoe Tycoon.

"It's what we've been telling you for two weeks," Reid reminded her. "Give the guy a chance. He isn't Brandon. He didn't do what he did because your nose wasn't high enough in the air for him."

Which was the general consensus of her family.

"And if his sister is okay with it," Ad contributed, "and you can make him see that your brothers toughened you up for him, he might surprise you."

Or he might just reject her a second time for the reason Cassie was still worried was the *real* reason...

Again she shook her head. "No. If he'd wanted to work things out with me he wouldn't have—"

"He's seriously more down than I've ever seen him," Alyssa said. "I think he wants you a lot."

"He didn't say that," Cassie insisted, feeling as if she were being steamrolled. And steamrolled into something that might pour salt into the wounds she already had.

"But he's my brother and I know him," Alyssa said. "Please? Go talk to him so I don't have to feel like I wrecked something good for him? You don't want me to have to go through the rest of my life thinking that I might be at fault for him never being happy, do you?"

The girl was amazingly adept at laying on the guilt.

Reid came to the table and took Cassie by the arm, half helping her up, half hoisting her. "Come on. I have my car. I'll drive you home, you can throw some things in a bag, and Ad will pick you up there to take you to Billings."

"I'll just let Kit know. Maybe she'll come with us," Ad said, referring to his wife.

Alyssa stood then, too. "I'll ride along and tell you how to beat security and then walk back to the dorm so you can pack."

"I'm not kidding," Cassie insisted forcefully. "This is not a good idea."

"It's a great idea," Reid said equally as forcefully, nearly dragging her through the restaurant. "Who knows Joshua better than his sister, and she suggested it. And you don't want her to spend the rest of her life carrying the burden of believing it was her fault that her brother didn't end up with who he was meant to be with, do you? No, you're going and that's all there is to it."

"I'm not chasing after him!" Cassie protested.

"You won't have to," Alyssa said confidently.

It wasn't a confidence Cassie shared and she couldn't help worrying that she was being pushed into a situation that might hurt her even more than she'd already been hurt because these well-meaning people didn't know the whole story.

But on the off chance that she'd been wrong, that Alyssa and Cassie's own family were right, Cassie let herself be pushed.

Chapter Sixteen

Maybe it was the fact that Cassie hadn't slept for more than two or three hours any night during the two weeks since Joshua had left.

Or maybe it was the fact that he'd rejected her and so she'd spent that time focusing on why—analyzing it, rehashing it, feeling bad about it.

Or maybe it was the fact that she'd felt so much better when his sister had made it seem as if rejecting her wasn't what he'd actually been inclined to do.

But as the taxi dropped her off where Alyssa had suggested, the reality of what Cassie was doing suddenly struck her.

She was in Los Angeles. In a suburb of the city where the houses—the estates—were like giant fortresses. And the Cantrell castle was the biggest among them.

A six-foot-high brick wall surrounded the grounds and only from a distance and due to the slight elevation of a hill as the cab had approached her destination had she been able to see the sprawling three-story Spanish-style house that Alyssa had told her belonged to Joshua.

The property encompassed at least a full city block. As Cassie stood alone on the sidewalk outside its confines at 1:00 a.m. on Saturday morning, she felt small and insignificant and very much the country bumpkin.

Which was probably why she had the reality check just then.

But whatever the reason, she asked herself what in the world she was doing there, wishing she'd listened more to her own misgivings about this idea and not let everyone else's enthusiasm drown them out.

It was just that Reid had driven Cassie and Alyssa to Cassie's house after leaving Ad's restaurant, cheering Cassie on and telling her she was absolutely doing the right thing by talking to Joshua—which had begun the process of muting her own hesitations.

Alyssa had helped her pack, and after outlining why Cassie couldn't just go to the front gate and announce herself to Joshua, had continued to encourage Cassie, seeming confident that Joshua would be thrilled to see her, and further burying Cassie's doubts.

Alyssa had left when Ad and Kit had shown up to whisk Cassie into Billings. On the drive her brother and sister-in-law had taken up the pep talk by elaborating on how much everyone liked Joshua, how down-to-earth he was, how unlike Brandon, how good Joshua and Cassie had seemed to be together.

And Cassie's own reasons against going to him had receded even more.

Cassie had barely made it to the airport in time to buy a ticket, get through security and board. Then she'd spent the flight continuously reminding herself of what Reid had said, of what Alyssa had said, of what Ad and Kit had said. And not allowing herself to consider the reason *she* would have nixed a future with Joshua herself had she had the chance—the reason being that they were very different people from very different worlds.

Only now, staring up at the brick wall that bordered his palatial estate, those differences had never been more glaring.

Cassie couldn't avoid thinking all over again that she didn't belong with Joshua Cantrell. That he'd likely realized that himself—just as Brandon had—only had tried to break it to her more gently by camouflaging it in not wanting to repeat his history or put her or Alyssa through the trauma that went with having a relationship with him.

Cassie could have kicked herself for having lost sight of those very, very important points and letting her heart rule her head.

"Idiot!" she whispered.

But what was she going to do now? She was out of range for her cell phone coverage. It was one o'clock in the morning in a suburban area. She'd already let her taxi drive off, and there was no way another one was going to just happen by for her to hail for a return trip to the airport.

She was stranded in other people's paradise. The quintessential fish out of water.

Briefly, she considered walking around to the front gate where Alyssa had said there were always at least three photographers camped out, hoping to catch sight of Joshua and/or whatever woman he was seeing at the time. She thought that she could make up a story that gave her no connection with Joshua and try to get the photographers to let her use one of their cell phones or to drive her to a convenience store to use a pay phone.

But after the horror stories about what jackals some of the photographers could be, and after Alyssa's warning that should Cassie go anywhere near them tonight she would be surrounded, photographed and hounded, Cassie was afraid of doing that. Who knew what questions they might ask of someone at this particular place, carrying a suitcase, in the middle of the night, or the type of people they might be. Who knew what kind of trouble she might get herself into.

Which left her with only one option: to do what Alyssa had told her to do so she could get up to the house unnoticed.

Yes, there would be awful, awkward questions from Joshua himself. Yes, she would be embarrassed beyond belief. And probably rejected all over again when he felt the need to confirm that he had, indeed, only been letting her down easy when in fact he didn't want her. But what else was she going to do at that point?

"Stupid, stupid idiot!" she said, wondering if sleep deprivation alone could make anyone as gullible as she felt at that moment for letting herself be pushed and prodded and persuaded against her better judgment by her own family and by an eighteen-year-old girl who felt guilty for something that probably wasn't her fault at all.

But there Cassie was, and she had no where else to turn.

She took a deep breath, sighed and—as instructed by Alyssa—counted the brick posts that stood between each wall.

Six from the corner—that was what Alyssa had said, so that was where Cassie headed. To the point that Alyssa had discovered was the only blind spot left by the security cameras where she could climb the outer wall and get onto the property without fanfare.

When she reached the sixth post she turned sideways to slip into the gap between two meticulously manicured bushes. And discovered that there really was a brick missing in the sixth post. About halfway up.

The suitcase was a problem. She didn't want to leave it hidden behind the bushes in case it was found while she was inside, opened and her personal and private things exposed for the press. So she took it to the front side of the bushes again, swung it a few times to gain momentum and threw it.

But that first attempt was a little short.

It hit the top of the wall with a thud and dropped to the ground behind the bushes.

Undaunted, Cassie retrieved it and tried a second time.

She made it on that attempt and, relieved, she turned and slipped between the bushes herself again.

Luckily she was dressed in jeans, a mock turtleneck sweater that zipped up the front and plain loafers—clothes easy to climb walls in—because now that she was about to do it, she could see that it wasn't going to be easy.

The gap left by the missing brick was about hip-high on her, but she managed to wedge her foot into it, push off with her other foot and lunge up to barely grab the ledge of the wall's capstone. Once she *was* up, she changed her grip to hang on to the decorative stone ball finial cemented atop the post.

That gave her the extra stability and leverage to swing her free foot over the wall. Then she lifted off with the missing-brick foot until she'd successfully made it to lie atop the twelve-inch wide capstone.

Which was when flood lights came on.

A deep, deadly serious voice boomed from inside the grounds. "Freeze!"

The photographers ran from around the corner, snapping pictures that flashed bright lights and blinded her as she lay flat on her stomach, straddling the wall and hugging the finial.

"Honestly, it's okay. I really do know her. She's not a stalker or anything. I'll take care of this. I don't need any help."

Cassie wondered if it wasn't an indication of how doomed this relationship was when the last time she'd been with Joshua she'd ended up hiding her face in her knees, and now here she was again, sitting on the bottom step of the enormous staircase that curved from his foyer up to the other two floors, with her face again pressed to the same spot, her arms once more hugging her shins.

She heard the security guards tell Joshua that if he changed his mind, they could still call the police and turn Cassie over as a trespasser. Only when he'd said he didn't think that would be necessary did they finally leave.

But the closing of the door behind them only meant she was now alone with Joshua, and Cassie wasn't too sure if being taken away like a criminal might not have been preferable.

"Well, hi," Joshua said then.

There didn't seem to be anger in his voice. Perplexity, perhaps. Puzzlement. Confusion. Certainly surprise. But not anger.

Cassie was grateful for that, anyway.

She steeled herself and sat up to look at him.

He was standing far across the foyer that was almost the size of her house. His back was against the now closed double doors. His feet and amazingly chiseled chest were bare. He was wearing only a pair of jeans he must have pulled on when all the commotion had rousted him out of bed. His hair was slightly longer and more tousled than the last time they'd been together, and there was the shadow of his beard adding another masculine, rugged, bad-boy air to him.

If Cassie had had only one wish at that moment, it would have been that he didn't look so incredible that it just made her want to throw herself into his arms.

But there he was and he *did* look incredible.

And it was as if a weight lifter were strangling the life out of her heart to know that this wasn't going to work out.

"I can't tell you how sorry I am," she said, the desperation in her tone adding weight to the words. "This was all crazy and I knew the minute the taxi drove off that I shouldn't have come. But it was too late to call another cab and there was nothing I could do except try to sneak in the way Alyssa told me to. But she said that was a blind spot in the security and I could do it without being seen and I guess that's not true and—"

"One of the security guys heard something hit the wall."

Her suitcase.

"I'm sorry," she repeated, forcing herself not to go on rambling now that Joshua had stopped her. "If you'll tell me where your phone is, I'll call for another taxi and get out of here."

"Without telling me what you're doing here in the first place?"

"It's too dumb to say. I just let Alyssa's guilt and my family's naiveté make me believe things I didn't—and *don't*—believe when I'm in my right mind. But I haven't slept and I've been… I just wasn't thinking straight. And then I saw this place and I knew, and now I'll go back to Northbridge."

"What did you know?"

"That we really are wrong for each other, you and I. That you know as well as Brandon did that that's true. That you were just being nice when you said you didn't want me because of what happened with Jennie."

"If you'll recall," he said quietly, "I said I *did* want you."

"You said it to sugarcoat the truth. It's okay. Honestly. Seeing this place—" She glanced around at a house she couldn't imagine living in. "Now I have the visual proof to remind me of just *how* wrong we are for each other."

"Let's back this up a little. What did you mean when you said *Alyssa's guilt?*"

"She asked me to have coffee with her today and told me…"

Cassie had been about to reveal what his sister had said about him but thought better of it.

"She told me that she'd been asking around about me and she'd taken into consideration the kind of person I am and she'd changed her mind. That she doesn't think I'm like Jennie and that maybe I could handle the stuff that goes on around you. It was actually Alyssa's idea for me to come here tonight. She outlined how to sneak in to avoid the photographers—which obviously I was rotten at—"

"And how did you like your first experience with the picture takers?"

"It was weird, that's for sure. And I can just imagine what the photographs will look like."

"Not to mention the captions that'll go with them."

"Cat Burglar Tries To Break Into Cantrell Estate?" she joked. "That'll make a new addition to my résumé. And my brothers will love it. They'll have the pictures blown up and framed by the time I get back. Ad will probably have one hanging in the restaurant. It'll take me at least a month to live it down."

But that was the least of her worries at that moment.

"Anyway," she continued, "Alyssa said you'd been…sort of in a bad mood since leaving Northbridge and she thought that if not being with me was the reason for that, she didn't want you keeping your distance because of her." Cassie waded cautiously through the territory she'd decided earlier to avoid.

Then she went from there.

"And I guess…I guess it was nice to hear and I let myself be convinced of things I shouldn't have. Things I know better than to believe. And then my family got in on it when Ad and Reid overheard what Alyssa had to say. They jumped on the bandwagon because they like you and they don't think you're like Brandon and…" She sighed, running out of steam. "And here I am."

"After not being able to sleep since I left?"

Oh good, pity. Just what she needed.

Cassie sighed. "It's no big deal."

"You don't think the pictures that were taken of you tonight and the fact that they'll probably be splashed all over the tabloids by tomorrow or the next day is a big deal, either."

Cassie shrugged. "I told you, my brothers will get a big kick out of it. So will most of Northbridge. I don't care about that." She stood and added, "I care about getting out of here now that you know the whole story and understand why I showed up on your doorstep. Or on your privacy wall, to be more accurate. I care about putting it all behind me. As far as I'm concerned, this is more embarrassing than any pictures could be. So, like I said, if you'll tell me where your phone is, I'll call for a taxi and go back to where I belong."

"Maybe you belong here."

Cassie glanced around her once more and laughed. "Right," she said facetiously. "Even Brandon's family's place would probably fit in your garage. If I didn't belong there, I definitely don't belong here."

"Your family doesn't think I'm another Brandon, so why do you keep hanging on to that idea?" Joshua asked.

"I agree, you're not another Brandon. It took me a while to realize that during the last two weeks. When I really thought about it, I couldn't find any financial or social similarities. You don't put on any airs. You don't think you're better than anyone. You're like one of the guys with my brothers and with everyone else in North-bridge." She looked around again. "But all this is not me. The supermodels and actresses and beauty queens you usually squire around? Also not me."

"Good," he proclaimed forcefully. "And that isn't *sugarcoating.*"

Then he pushed off the door and started across the expansive foyer.

Initially Cassie thought he was going to lead her to his telephone.

But instead, he stopped in front of her. Very close to her.

"And if Alyssa said I was just in some generic bad mood, she was covering for me because I've been in-consolably miserable and crabby and short-tempered and I haven't been sleeping worth a damn, either."

Cassie raised her gaze to his face, refusing to hope this was going where it suddenly seemed to be.

"You see," Joshua continued, "what I discovered during these last two weeks was that I didn't only want you. I'm in love with you. Madly in love with you. Which, when I figured I couldn't have you, made me furious with myself for letting it happen. It made me a little annoyed even with Alyssa for being afraid you were just another Jennie and getting me to worry about the same thing and deny myself what I wanted most. And, to tell you the truth, it also made me a little annoyed with you and fate and the whole universe because you *aren't* someone who's been in the limelight and knows how to handle it. But I have to say, you did pretty well for yourself tonight. No doubt one of the pictures that gets printed will be of you waving to the photographers as we got you down from that wall."

Cassie laughed but grimaced at that memory. "I probably shouldn't have done that."

"They loved it. I loved it. I also loved that instead of fretting about it just now, you don't think it's a big deal. That you can make jokes about it and don't care if other people do. That you can take it in stride. So maybe I was off base to think that your family wouldn't be able to handle it, too. Even if something like Ben's sordid teenage history comes out."

Joshua took both of her upper arms in his hands. "Maybe you—and the rest of your family—just aren't as fragile as Jennie was."

Cassie had to roll her eyes at that. "*Fragile?* My brothers would be insulted if they heard you say that. I told you—they saw it as their job to toughen me up so I wouldn't be so much of a *girl*."

Joshua smiled. "I'm grateful they weren't *too* successful at that. But I was still worried—until seeing you out there tonight—that they hadn't toughened you up enough."

"And now you *aren't* worried anymore?"

"Let's say that I'm *less* worried. Like, after talking to Alyssa last night I got a little less worried about her concerns over you and I being together."

He squeezed her arms. "So maybe," he said then, "it's beginning to look like the obstacles might not be obstacles after all. Yours or mine. And if that's the case, then I'd say that you're mistaken about us being wrong for each other. That we're actually just the opposite of that or it wouldn't have taken one lousy Parents' Week to make this happen between us."

"Are you saying that it's *not* such a bad thing that I came?" Cassie asked quietly, tentatively, wanting desperately to know if that was the case.

"Actually, I was thinking that it's an absolutely *great* thing that you came. Especially since it gave me the chance to *see* you handle the press, and then to *see* the aftereffects—which seem to be minimal." He paused and then added, "Uh, at least it's all a great thing if you feel about me the way I feel about you…."

Cassie grinned, knowing she was flashing him the dimples he liked. "If I'm in love with you, too?"

"Those would be the feelings, yeah."

"I guess it's a great thing that I came, then."

"Because you're madly in love with me?"

"Because I'm so madly in love with you that I can hardly stand it."

Joshua grinned in return. "Then I guess since it was Alyssa's idea that got you onto my privacy wall, she's earned her whole four years tuition for it—that's how great a thing it is that you came."

His expression turned slightly more serious again. "Although, I think you should also know that I can't imagine spending the rest of my life without you. I haven't been able to imagine it for two weeks—which was another reason I've been a bear to be anywhere near. And now that I have you here, I'm not letting you go."

He pulled her to him as if to prove that, kissing her with an eagerness, a hunger, born of separation and what seemed like the same kind of despair Cassie had felt during the last two weeks when she'd believed it was over with him.

That was good, too, though. She kissed him back the same way. She let her arms snake up under his, laid her hands on his back and hung on hard, absorbing the feel of that big body that she'd thought she'd never feel again.

And in that instant, passion—hot and fiery—ignited. A passion so combustible, so intense it wouldn't be denied. It wouldn't even be delayed.

Not that either of them tried because right there, in the well-lit entry of Joshua's gargantuan house, he unzipped the front zipper that closed her sweater and peeled it off her. And suddenly Cassie was oblivious to where they were. To everything but Joshua and her own needs.

Without thought of anything else, she kicked off her shoes and socks. He unfastened her jeans and she unfastened his and they were flung aside in tandem, followed close behind by her bra and panties.

And once they were free of the confines of clothes, Joshua lifted her up onto the table against the wall near the staircase and let his mouth and his hands reacquaint themselves with every inch of her.

With breasts that were swelled with the demand for his attention.

With nipples that were so tight they almost hurt for want of his mouth on them.

With pulling her against that part of him that left no question that he was as hot for her as she was for him.

That part of him that found its home inside of her right there on that table in his foyer, with her legs wrapped around his hips and her hands going from his hair to his thick neck to his biceps to his own male nibs before all she could do was cling to his back as, together, their passion soared to its peak.

And only when it—and they—were spent and slaked, when Joshua was holding her tightly to him, when Cassie's head was resting weakly on his shoulder, did it occur to her to wonder if photographers or security guards or anyone else could be witnessing this.

"Oh my gosh, is anyone else here? Can anyone see us from outside?" she asked, her alarm ringing in her voice.

Joshua chuckled, a deep, raspy laugh. "That *would* be bad. But no, no one else is here and everything is designed so no one can see in."

Cassie raised her head only enough to peek and make sure he was telling her the truth. Which he seemed to be.

"Still, I don't think this is advisable for the future," she said, laying her head back on his shoulder and kissing the side of his neck.

"Maybe not. But the master bedroom is on the third

floor and not even the elevator would have gotten us there fast enough."

"You have an elevator in your house?"

"Two. But I never use them."

Cassie laughed. "My brothers are going to have a field day with this when I tell them."

"About the elevators or this?" he asked, pulsing inside of her.

"I don't think I'll be telling them about this." She flexed back.

"How about if we don't tell them about the elevators, either, and just let them discover them for themselves when they visit?"

"Visit?" she repeated, not trying to be coy, just not wanting to make any assumptions.

"When we're in L.A. they'll visit us, won't they?"

"Will there be an *us?*"

"There will be if you say you'll marry me. Otherwise, they'll have to storm the place to try to rescue you—I told you, I'm not letting you go."

"And they'll need elevators for the rescue?" she teased.

"It's the only way to get to the dungeon."

Cassie laughed and pushed into him once again. "Maybe I'd just like to *see* the dungeon," she said with a voice full of innuendo.

"Why don't you let me show you the bedroom first? Where, by the way, my bags are packed because I was headed back to Northbridge tomorrow to talk to you, to try to hash through everything and see if Alyssa was right and maybe you *could* handle what comes with being with me."

That pleased Cassie enough to make her grin even as he slipped out of her and put a scant inch between them.

"Really? You were coming to see me? If I had just waited a day it would have been you chasing after me instead of me chasing after you?"

"It would have been," he confirmed.

"And you waited until *now* to tell me?" she said, feigning anger she just couldn't muster.

He returned her grin as his only answer before he delved into her eyes with his brilliant silver-gray ones and said, "But I'm only showing you the master bedroom if you give me an answer."

"To..."

"To whether or not you'll marry me."

She might have pretended to mull it except that without the warmth of his body she was getting cold. "I think I will," she said as if it didn't require any thought at all.

And actually, it didn't.

Because as Joshua kissed her again to seal the pact, and then scooped her from the table into his arms to carry her—naked—up the stairs, Cassie knew that wherever Joshua was was where she belonged. Whether in Northbridge or Los Angeles or any far-flung corner of the world.

She knew, too—with certainty and clarity now—that he really was the everyday guy he'd seemed to be. An everyday guy who just happened to be caught up in an abnormal situation. He wasn't like Brandon at all, regardless of whether or not they moved in similar circles.

He didn't have the same attitudes or opinions or arrogance. He didn't have the same views or feelings when it came to anything, let alone to her. He didn't think he was better than anyone, despite all that he'd achieved. And that was why he'd fit in so well in Northbridge and with her family.

That was why he was truly just right for her.

And not only was Joshua just right for her.

She also knew that she was just right for him.

And always would be.

* * * * *

Look for Victoria Pade's next
NORTHBRIDGE NUPTIALS *book*
*in August 2006, where the mystery surrounding
the recently discovered duffel bag and its connection
to a decades-old robbery will raise even more
questions for this tight-knit community!*

This riveting new saga begins with

In the Dark

by national bestselling author

JUDITH ARNOLD

The party at Hotel Marchand is in full swing when the lights suddenly go out. What does head of security Mac Jensen do first? He's torn between two jobs—protecting the guests at the hotel and keeping the woman he loves safe.

A woman to protect. A hotel to secure. And no idea who's determined to harm them.

On Sale June 2006

Page-turning drama...

Exotic, glamorous locations...

Intense emotion and passionate seduction...

Sheikhs, princes and billionaire tycoons...

This summer, may we suggest:

THE SHEIKH'S DISOBEDIENT BRIDE
by Jane Porter

On sale June.

AT THE GREEK TYCOON'S BIDDING
by Cathy Williams

On sale July.

THE ITALIAN MILLIONAIRE'S VIRGIN WIFE

On sale August.

With new titles to choose from every month,
discover a world of romance in our books written
by internationally bestselling authors.

HARLEQUIN *Presents*

It's the ultimate in quality romance!

Available wherever Harlequin books are sold.

www.eHarlequin.com

HPGEN06

**Hidden in the secrets of antiquity,
lies the unimagined truth...**

Introducing

a brand-new line filled with mystery
and suspense, action and adventure,
and a fascinating look into history.
And it all begins with DESTINY.

In a sealed crypt in
France, where the
terrifying legend of
the beast of Gevaudan
begins to unravel,
Annja Creed discovers
a stunning artifact
that will seal her destiny.

*Available every other
month starting
July 2006, wherever
you buy books.*

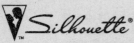

SPECIAL EDITION

#1765 THE RELUCTANT CINDERELLA—Christine Rimmer
Talk of the Town

When humble business owner Megan Schumacher landed the Banning's department store account, she landed Greg Banning, too. He loved her ideas for updating the company's image—and couldn't get the image of this sexy woman out of his head. But the town gossips had a field day—and Greg's ex-wife, who'd introduced the pair, *wasn't* amused....

#1766 PRINCESS IN DISGUISE—Lilian Darcy
Wanted: Outback Wives

Tired of her philandering fiancé, jet-setting Princess Misha decided to unwind at a remote sheep farm in Australia. But when she arrived, farmer Brant Smith mistook her for one of the candidates a local woman's magazine had been sending him as a possible wife! Perhaps the down-to-earth royal fit the bill more than either of them first suspected....

#1767 THE BABY TRAIL—Karen Rose Smith
Baby Bonds

Finding a stranger's baby in her sunroom, Gwen Longworthy resolved to reunite mother and child, since she knew all too well the pain of separation. Luckily she had former FBI agent Garrett Maxwell to help search for the mother...and soothe Gwen's own wounded heart.

#1768 THE TENANT WHO CAME TO STAY—Pamela Toth
Reunited

Taking in male boarder Wade Garrett was a stretch for Pauline Mayfield—falling in love with him really turned heads! And just when Pauline had all the drama she could take, her estranged sister, Lily, showed up, with child in tow and nowhere to go. The more the merrier...or would Lily get up to her old tricks and make a play for Pauline's man?

#1769 AT THE MILLIONAIRE'S REQUEST—Teresa Southwick

When millionaire Gavin Spencer needed a speech therapist for his injured son, he asked for M. J. Taylor's help. But the job reminded M.J. of the tragic loss of her own child, and her proximity to Gavin raised trust issues for them both. As the boy began to heal, would M.J. and Gavin follow suit—and give voice to their growing feelings for each other?

#1770 SECOND-TIME LUCKY—Laurie Paige
Canyon Country

How ironic that family counselor Caileen Peters had so much trouble keeping her own daughter in line. And that Caileen was turning to her client Jefferson Aquilon, a veteran raising two orphans, for help. But mother and daughter both found inspiration in the Aquilon household—and Caileen soon found something more in Jefferson's arms.

SSECNM0604